A Taste of Northern Spies
A Dorothea Montgomery Mystery

by
Elizabeth Jukes

For information, email Cozy Cat Press, cozycatpress@aol.com or visit our website at: www.cozycatpress.com

COZY CAT
PRESS

ISBN: 978-1-946063-87-8
Printed in the United States of America

10 9 8 7 6 5 4 3 2 1

Dedication

In memory of Terrina Rehkopf who, delightfully, did not take herself too seriously and lifted the burden from those who did.

Chapter One

Dorothea Montgomery was a brisk walker and a
brisk thinker and right now she was doing both. She
had been busy indoors throughout the day with
household responsibilities and the May day had not
tempted her outside because it wholly lived up to the
capriciousness of a Canadian spring with drizzle and
even some moments of sleet. For the past three days the
breezes had been balmy, coaxing crabapple trees to
plump out their buds but today… "rough windes do
shake the darling buds of Maie" as Shakespeare phrased
it. However, now—this evening—she couldn't stay
inside one more minute no matter the state of
precipitation. As she marched along in her snug wool
coat, galoshes firmly snapped over her shoes and
umbrella defiantly standing up for her against cold,
sleety rain, she intended to think out all the thoughts
that had to be set aside throughout the day's tasks. She
would head out to the other side of town, past
Willowsdown's train depot by a block or two and then
return by a block or two on the other side of the depot.
With her route mapped out, she stepped smartly along.
In the dusk no one else was out and about. The wind
gusted about halfheartedly as though it was ready to go
to bed but just needed a few more minutes and it tugged
a strand of Dorothea's silvery hair. She tucked it behind
her ear. She wondered if she should get her hair cut in a
bob, which was all the rage. Her troop of Girl Guides
assured her it would make her life easier. She liked
rolling her silvering hair into a bun at the back because

it revealed the last vestige of her youth—a jet patch at the nape of her neck always saw the light of day in the old style and she admitted ruefully to herself that she was proud of that glimpse of bygone days. As she mused on the nonsensical vagaries of vanity and fashion, she heard in the distance a faint shout that sounded like "Stop!" Or maybe it was "Spot!" as someone called their dog. She had decided not to bring Lily, her Bichon Frise, on this walk as Lily had spent most of the day chasing squirrels in the yard. Not, as Dorothea knew, in order to frighten the squirrels but rather so as to make friends with them. Lily wanted to be friends with everything. Dorothea's husband, Charles, suggested that Lily might like to doze by a small fire and dream of happy times playing with her squirrel friends.

Anyway, Dorothea thought curtly to herself, *get your thoughts in order.* The one situation she most wanted to mull over was the Elva and George question. It had surfaced today at teatime when she was paging through magazines. She was spying out ads suitable for cutting into geometric shapes. The sliced up adverts would be placed into separate envelopes and presented as puzzles to her grandchildren the next time they visited. So far, ads for Wrigley's chewing gum, a scooter, a baby Dimples doll, and Canada Dry ginger ale all made entirely suitable puzzle fodder. Also an ad for a Louis Armstrong record—she would throw that in for Charles who so enjoyed Mr. Armstrong's music. Turning a page she had come across patterns for bridesmaids' dresses for the weddings of 1927. She had sighed and gazed unseeingly out the window at the gray day. For about six weeks during December and January, her sister, Edith, and Edith's grandchildren, Alice and George, had visited from England, all becoming embroiled in an upset surrounding the theft of a brooch belonging to

Edith, and the suspicious death of a townsman. But when Edith and Alice returned to England, George had stayed in Willowsdown, taking a job at Charles' insurance company. It wasn't, however, the job that kept him here. It was the whip smart, plumply petite, Elva North who worked at the telegraph/phone exchange office. In March, Elva and George became engaged and Elva began planning for a June wedding. But two weeks ago, she broke off the engagement. Evidently, George could not understand why Elva wanted to continue working at the exchange office after their marriage. She was adamant and he was bewildered. Charles had met with George that afternoon but what he said to George, Dorothea couldn't imagine. A woman who was marrying a very financially secure fellow and still choosing to work was decidedly uncharted territory for Charles. She knew it was none of her business; her great nephew and his fiancée were adults and needed to sort it all out themselves but she did want to wrap her mind around it.

And then there was the matter of the paper that Dianna had brought to her attention. Dianna was a young woman who had worked full time as house help in the Montgomery household for several years but had recently acquired a part-time position in the housekeeping department at The Imperial, Willowsdown's largest hotel. Dianna's grandmother had been lady's maid to Dorothea's mother so Dianna seemed more one of the family than staff. The conversation with Dianna had taken place after dinner as Dorothea was attending to the household accounts at her desk in the Morning Room.

Dianna had said, "I need to show you something that I found this morning during my shift at the Imperial. Mrs. White told me to hop to it and then get back to my duties."

In the midst of her ambulatory musings, Dorothea realized that her right hand was chilled from holding the umbrella. She pulled a pair of gloves from her coat pocket, tucking the open umbrella under her arm as she tugged the gloves on. Umbrella in place again, she smiled to herself as she remembered Dianna's words. Mrs. White was the cook at the Montgomery house. There was no doubt that she prepared and presented mouthwatering meals and was rightfully well known for her culinary delights but she was just as well known for the bossiness with which she treated all those under her watchful eye.

"What is it?" Dorothea had asked.

"It's this envelope that I found while I was cleaning one of the rooms."

Dianna had handed Dorothea a manila envelope and Dorothea unwound the string from the button. "I showed the manager but he said it looked like a geography project and probably wasn't important. I wasn't sure I should get rid of it so I brought it to you."

Dorothea had squinted myopically at the paper in front of her, murmuring, "I think I need reading glasses."

A foolscap sheet of paper was covered in even handwriting. It seemed to be outlining the geographical whereabouts of bridges, train tracks and depots and various roads—in Vermont.

"Who was staying in the room where you found this?" Dorothea had asked.

"Some military fellow. He wore a uniform. Young, light brown hair. He had been at the hotel for I think a little over two weeks but mostly kept to his room. I took a pen to him once. He was polite and the room was as neat as a pin," replied Dianna.

"Hmm, yes, military training. I've seen him around town but his uniform is Canadian. This information, though, is clearly stated to be from Vermont. Strange that he left this behind as it seems incomplete. Do you see, Dianna, how at the top of the page it begins mid-sentence and also at the bottom? There must be more pages. Good thinking on your part, my dear, not to dispose of it. Once he realizes he's missing a page, he'll likely be back." Dorothea had slid the sheet into the envelope and the envelope between two books on a top shelf of the bookcase over her desk. "It will keep well enough there in case he does return."

So, two returnings: would the military fellow return for his sheet of foolscap listing co-ordinates and details of bridges, train tracks and depots and roads in Vermont, of all places, and would Elva and George return to each other? She had been walking and thinking for over half an hour and was on her return journey. Dusk had deepened into a slate gray dark. Dorothea approached the train track where she thought she could see a bundle of something beside the track. Had someone thrown a large parcel from the train? She recalled the episode in December when Bill Wainfleet, the stationmaster, had discovered jars of beef broth beside the track. That discovery had, improbable as it seemed at the time, led to the culprits behind the theft of Dorothea's sister's brooch. This parcel though looked much much bulkier. Because of the deepening dark, Dorothea was almost on top of the "bundle of something" before she realized what it was.

"Joe!" she exclaimed, tossing her umbrella aside and kneeling beside the crumpled form of the town's constable. She touched his face and his hand. They were cold.

"Joe!" she said again, urgently, rubbing his right hand between her gloved hands. He was lying on his left side with a bloodied head but he was breathing—barely, it seemed to Dorothea. She heard footsteps behind her. Apprehensively she turned her head towards them.

"Mrs. Montgomery! Is that you?" called the voice of Bill Wainfleet, the stationmaster.

"Oh, Mr. Wainfleet, thank goodness," breathed Dorothea with relief.

"What's all this?" asked Mrs. Wainfleet as the couple came to stand beside Dorothea. "Why, it's Joe North! Whatever has happened?"

"I've no idea," replied Dorothea. "I've just come upon him myself. He must have been lying here for some time. He's very cold and he hasn't responded at all. We've got to get him inside. Do you think the three of us could carry him to your house?"

The train track ran parallel to a street and on the other side of that street, a streetlight beside the stationmaster's house suffused the yellow brick with a welcoming warmth.

"We could," replied Mrs. Wainfleet, "but I'm not sure we should. He's very cold as you say," she continued, touching his exposed hand. "Let me get blankets and call Dr. Payne. I've nursed, as you know, and moving someone can be risky business. Start by covering him with your coats," she called over her shoulder as she headed to the Wainfleet house.

"Yes, yes, she's absolutely right," remarked Dorothea to Mr. Wainfleet as she unbuttoned her coat and unwound her scarf.

"She's a good 'un, all right is my Anna," said Bill Wainfleet, tucking his overcoat over Joe's legs while Dorothea lay her coat over his arms and torso and wrapped her scarf gently around his head.

She knelt beside Joe and reached for her discarded umbrella to shelter him as best she could when she realized that there was no precipitation to shield him from. Sometime in the last few minutes the sleety rain had ceased.

"We was out to supper down the road and just on our ways home when we saw you," explained Bill, hunkering down on the other side of Joe, both of them with the thought of adding whatever warmth their proximity could give him. They each rubbed their arms against the damp chill.

"I'm very glad you did. I've been out walking for half an hour and I've seen no one. Not surprising, of course, in this weather."

"Good thing he fell 'side the track and not on it 'cause if no one had found him, the 9:55 might not've seen him in time. What was he stumbling 'round the track for anyway? It's not as though Joe's a drinking man."

Dorothea shuddered at Bill's observation. It had been known to happen. With or without Prohibition there were still those who drank too much and in wandering home in a stupor had tripped over the train track, lain where they fell and been killed by an oncoming train. She couldn't imagine that was the case with Joe. They sat in shivery silence for a few minutes waiting for Anna Wainfleet. The Wainfleet front door slammed and they saw Anna rushing down the porch steps loaded with blankets. Standing up from their squatting positions they shook out their wobbly legs and moved toward Anna.

"Bill!" cried Anna as she hurried across the street. "Bill! We've been burgled!"

"Burgled!" Dorothea and Bill exclaimed together, meeting Anna in the middle of the street and each plucking a blanket from her arms.

"Someone has been in the house AND your bike is gone. Dr. Payne said he'll be 'round immediately. Cover Joe right up and tuck under him as much as possible. That's right. The scarf 'round his head was a good idea, Mrs. Montgomery. You two go in the house where it's warm. I'll stay with Joe until Dr. Payne comes. And, Bill, look 'round and see what's missing."

"Did you call Chief Goodman?" asked Dorothea.

"Didn't want to take the time," Anna replied.

"I'll call him while you look around, Bill. Anna, I'll leave you the umbrella just in case."

"Before you do anything, get the kettle on, Bill, so's you and Mrs. Montgomery can have some tea."

"Righto, m'dear. I make a grand cup of tea, Mrs. Montgomery. We'll be warm in no time. I'll bring one out to you, love."

Dorothea had looped the lace curtain behind the heavier drape in the front window of the Wainfleet's living room so that she had a clear view of the accident scene. She cupped her hot tea and peered out the window where she could make out the forms of people moving about. Besides Mrs. Wainfleet, she recognized the slightly stooped figure of the town's aging Dr. Payne. She pressed her nose against the glass. It looked to her as though Elva was also there. Elva and Joe were sister and brother. And ... yes, that was Ambrose North, grandfather of Elva and Joe and the town's baker. Someone else was running up the street from behind the huddled group. It was George! She supposed that despite everything that had happened between them, Elva must have notified him.

As she watched the proceedings of the group around Joe, her mind retrieved the newspaper headline from a few days previously. "Hot chase thru streets of city ends in arrest of two swift beer runners." It was whispered—well, more than whispered—that a distillery and brewery in the main town of the neighbouring county, had been contributing to the illegal sale of alcohol in the United States. It was legal to make spirits and beer but not to sell it. It was also legal to export it but not into countries with Prohibition. Countries such as their southern neighbour. Dorothea was not so naive as to believe that in her gentle Willowsdown that there weren't stills around. Maybe Joe saw something suspicious. Apparently, very often the police came up short in these car chases because the whiskey runners' average looking vehicles hid powerful engines that left police cars far behind. Except, it would seem, in the chase recently headlined. *I wonder what kind of car the Waterloo police have?* she thought. Maybe Chief Goodman should look into that. In Joe's case, if it was a case, a car might have been the thing he needed. *A bit far-fetched,* she told herself. She concentrated instead on the group's gesturing and nodding and was just going to head outside again when she saw George sprinting toward the house. She got up to open the door to him.

"Aunt Dot. Doctor wants some kind of board to lay Joe on. Mrs. Wainfleet said if there's nothing else, they could remove a door. Is Mr. Wainfleet around?"

"He's in the kitchen with Chief Goodman. Where does the doctor want Joe?"

"At home," said George shortly on his way to the kitchen.

Ten minutes later, an odd procession traversed the two blocks to the North home. The door to the Wainfleet's basement had been removed and Joe carefully transferred onto it. He still hadn't responded in any way. Three of the corners were carried by Joe's grandfather, Ambrose North; George Seyler, Dorothea's grandnephew (and recently Elva North's fiancée); and Bill Wainfleet. The fourth corner was supported by Dr. Payne and Elva North. While the group made their solemn way, Mrs. Wainfleet took the teacup offered by Dorothea and said, "Dr. Payne's quite sure there's no spinal damage. It seems to be solely a head injury. There was a sharp rock near his head with blood on it. The doctor is thinking that somehow Joe tripped and fell hard on that rock."

Tripped, thought Dorothea, *or was he hit with it?* Since someone had obviously been up to no good in rummaging in the Wainfleets' house and stealing Bill's bike, had Joe and that person come to blows?

Chief Goodman tromped down the stairs from the second floor and into the living room. "Can't see anything out of order myself, Mrs. Wainfleet, but you and Bill be sure to take a good looking over and report back to me."

"We will. I looked about a bit but I can't see anything missing on this floor; except, of course, for Bill's bike which he always keeps just inside the hallway by the back door."

"Well, we can do some more looking tomorrow by the light of day."

"That'll be fine. Would you like some tea, Chief?"

"No thanks, Mrs. Wainfleet. Think I'll just trot over to the Norths' before I head home and make sure Joe is settled."

"And I need to be heading home too," said Dorothea. "Would you mind giving me a ring when you get home, Chief? I'd be happy to hear about Joe."

"Right. Good night, ladies," he said slapping his wool cap onto his bald head.

Chapter Two

Early in the morning of the following day the sky
continued leaden but by mid-morning it matched the
colour of the robin's eggs in the nests atop the pillars on
Dorothea's front porch. Charles used to pile rocks on
the pillar tops to discourage the birds from making
nests as they left such a mess on the porch floor but
generations of intrepid robins had simply arranged
themselves on the rocks so Charles conceded defeat. As
a young boy, their son, Leland, always wanted to be
lifted up to see the blue eggs and then the baby birds.
Given their diminutive size, the baby birds could send
up a tremendous clamour when waiting to be fed. They
were doing it now. Dorothea was digging the spent tulip
bulbs from the flowerbed in front of the porch. She
gazed hungrily at the tiny green pearls on the stalks of
the lilies-of-the-valley. They were her absolute
favourite flower and every spring she eagerly awaited
their appearance. She sat back on her haunches and
sang, "White coral bells, upon a slender stalk, lilies-of-
the-valley deck my garden walk. Oh, don't you wish
that you might hear them ring. That will happen only
when the fairies sing."

"That will happen only when the fairies sing,"
repeated a somewhat out of tune voice.

"Edwina," said Dorothea, warmly getting up a little
stiffly. As always, her closest friend, Edwina Quayle,
was dressed in the latest style with a cloche hat pulled
snugly over her bobbed hair. No old-fashioned-hair-
rolled-at-the-back-of-the-head for her. "Where are you
off to?"

"To you. Where else? I heard it was you who found Joe North. Do you want help?"

"I only have the one trowel with me. Dilman and the hired boy are using the others in the back gardens." She didn't bother mentioning that Edwina was hardly dressed for kneeling on the damp ground and digging in the dirt. She knew there was no point as Edwina always put her hand to whatever task presented itself regardless of the ruin to her raiment.

"Well, then," said Edwina. "How long have you been working? Is it time for a break?"

"I just have this last cluster to dig up. Go sit on the porch; I can hear you from there. As long, that is, as those babies have full tummies." Dorothea waved in the direction of the robin's nest.

"Those robins are back again. Amazing. How long has Dilman been working? Do you think he may be ready for a snack break? If Mrs. White is too busy, I could carry a tray out to them."

Dorothea bent to her task in order to hide her grin. The Lucky Strike cigarettes' slogan was "reach for a Lucky instead of a sweet," and about six months ago Edwina had taken up smoking to do just that. However, she was entirely inconsistent about it and would often introduce the idea of a "snack" for someone else and just happen to include herself in it. Dilman White was married to Betty White, the Montgomery household cook. He was the gardener/odd job/chauffeur for the Montgomerys and as thin as a rail. No matter how many of Mrs. White's cream puffs or butter tarts or her apple pies made with northern spy apples or, at this time of the year, rhubarb pies Dilman ate, he remained thin. Much to Edwina's envy and disgust.

"Don't worry about Dilman; Mrs. White takes good care of him. Not sure where he's at in terms of a break but I'll be ready for one when I'm done with this. I'm sure Mrs. White can rustle us up something."

"Oh, I really don't need anything. I'll just reach for a Lucky while I'm waiting for you. Now," she pronounced, after lighting a cigarette, "I think we won't be able to sit out here for long: it's just a bit too chilly. No wonder Joe North is in a fever after lying out in that rain last evening."

"He's in a fever?"

"Yes. I was at the telegraph office this morning sending a telegram and Elva told me."

"Has he said anything?"

"Nothing. Evidently he's hardly moved."

Dorothea frowned as she tucked the last tulip bulb into her basket. She didn't like the sound of this. Her Leland, the one who used to thrill to the sound of the baby birds, had died almost thirteen years ago from a blow to the head.

Edwina continued, "Elva said Dr. Payne was there this morning and seemed more concerned about the fever than the head injury."

Dorothea knew her friend had read her mind.

"And," Edwina exhaled cigarette smoke, "Chief Goodman found Bill Wainfleet's bike at the back of a neighbour's house."

"At a neighbour's? That's odd."

"No need to get all suspicious, Dorothea. I'm sure there's a simple explanation. Bill is happy to have his bike back."

Dorothea thought about her theory of illegal alcohol sales. *Did whiskey runners use bikes?*

"Well, if someone did steal it, he isn't a very effective thief. There! That's got that job done. Shall we see what Mrs. White has in the larder?"

Edwina waved her cigarette in apparent nonchalance but her eyes brightened.

In the meantime Chief Goodman was checking on alibis. There were a couple of fellows who had come to Chief Goodman's attention as law enforcer in the last few years; he wanted to know where they had been the previous evening.

Dr. Caleb Oswald Winthrow was the town's vet. He had kindly offered to take the one fellow on as an apprentice so the chief's first stop was the vet clinic.

"Good morning, May," said Chief Goodman. "Is the doc in?"

"No sorry, Nelson, he's out on a call."

"Is young Sam with him?"

"He is."

"Drat. I don't suppose you have any idea when they'll be back?"

"No. You know how it goes—there's no guaranteed end time. Hopefully it won't go on too long as they had a late night last night."

Chief Goodman perked up.

"They did? As in both of them?"

"Yes."

"How long were they out?"

"Mmm, well, they were called out to the Harris farm around 4:30 p.m. and by the time Caleb dropped off Sam, I would say it was 11:30 p.m. before he dropped into bed."

"Thanks, May, I won't need to speak with Sam after all. You've been a great help."

"Oh. All right. Not sure how, but glad to be of service."

The chief saluted her. His next stop was Isaac Kingswood's blacksmith shop. His other possible delinquent was working there part time. The townspeople were rallying around the fatherless young man by offering him training in different career options.

Bill Wainfleet had also taken him underwing to see if life as a stationmaster might one day appeal to him.

Isaac and Philip had each finished quenching their piece of work and had stepped outside into the sunshine reaching for a Coca Cola from the ice box that stood just outside the shop door. There wasn't much point in putting it in the shop as the heat from the forge would make the ice obsolete in no time.

"Good morning, Chief." Isaac put out a blackened hand and Chief Goodman tried not to wince at the vise-like grip. "Would you like a bottle?" asked Isaac, nodding towards the ice box.

"No thanks, Isaac, but I would like a word with Philip here."

Chief Goodman led Philip to just around a corner of the shop. "Now, son, I'd like you to tell me where you were last evening between 5:00 p.m. and 7:30 p.m.?"

"At 5:00 I was just leaving the shop. I went right home," came the gruff answer.

"What were you doing while at home?"

"My mom and me and the kids ate supper. I chopped some wood and went to bed early. Mr. Kingswood had needed me into work early yesterday morning. It had been a long day. I was tired."

"All right, thank you, Philip. Enjoy your cola."

If Philip's mother vouched for him then that would be that. No one knew about the rummaging in the Wainfleets' house so she wouldn't be on her guard. One wanted to believe that a mother would be objective on a point of justice but the odds were more likely that she would come down on the side of her child.

As it turned out, Philip's alibi was guilelessly corroborated by a sibling who not being quite well that morning had been allowed to stay home from school. The whole story of the family's previous evening was told from the perspective of the suffering one as the illness had begun sometime after school and how it affected each family member was related. So he was back to square one. He had no idea who had entered the Wainfleet home or why.

It was while she and Edwina were enjoying a cup of tea and a biscuit smothered with last year's strawberry jam that Dorothea remembered the American family. Their arrival at The Imperial a few weeks ago had caused quite a stir in the small town of Willowsdown. She had heard of it first from Mrs. Johnson of The Grocery Emporium.

"Oh, Mrs. Montgomery! Have you been elucidated as to the appearance of some American tourists in our town?"

Mr. and Mrs. Johnson were the hard-working couple who owned the town's grocery store which in some ways served as the social centre for the community. Mrs. Johnson reveled in rolling her tongue around what could be considered less than normal run-of-the-mill words and with these she shared any social tidbits forthwith.

"I just heard something about it at George Flesherton's butcher shop: a mother and father and their grown daughter."

"Exactly so! Here for a few weeks, I understand," Mrs. Johnson had offered.

Reminded of this, it occurred to Dorothea that maybe the information about Vermont tucked in a book on her bookcase might make some sense to them. She would send Dilman to The Imperial with her card and see if she could call on them later. In the meantime, she needed to hunt up a simple cookie recipe for her Girl Guides' pack. With the upcoming Victoria Day parade and evening fireworks it seemed to her to be a perfect opportunity for the Guides to bake and sell cookies as a way of making money for this summer's camping trip. If she was able to visit with the American family she would stop by Ambrose North's bake shop and see what he would suggest.

A card from a Mrs. Robert Roberts arrived after dinner with the message that she would be at the hotel this afternoon and very happy to receive Mrs. Montgomery. Dorothea headed out in time to pop by the bake shop and still be on time for Mrs. Roberts. She stepped over the shop's threshold. The contrast of the cool freshness of a May day with the yeasty warmth of the shop's interior made her tingle with the delight of being alive. The North family had been supplying Willowsdown and the surrounding area with bread and rolls for two generations. Every morning the delivery truck was stuffed with loaves and trundled to the train station where its contents were loaded onto the train to be delivered to the various depots along the track. New to the inventory in the last few years were cakes, cookies, pies and—Dorothea's favourite—cinnamon buns. Elva and Joe's grandfather, Ambrose North, the bakery's founder still kept his hand, literally, in the business although nowadays most of the work was done by employees. He was a tall man with a white bristling moustache and twinkling eyes. He knew everyone's name and their favourite kind of bread. He didn't just sell bread, the staple of life, his enthusiasm infused life into the staple. Today though, something was not right. She sniffed tension in the air. One customer was leaving with her mouth set in a straight line and Ambrose North was apologizing profusely to another customer because, it seemed, her order was not ready.

Dorothea was flabbergasted. Orders not ready! That never happened. The second customer headed to the door and yet a third was told that she too would have to return for her order. As the third unhappy woman left, Dorothea approached the counter and smiled at the weary man behind it.

"Something's not right, Mr. North. What is it?"

Ambrose North sighed and wiped his hands on his apron. "Kind of you to ask, Mrs. Montgomery. With Joe being injured you know, we were already left short one person to come in early and work on the bread but then this morning one of my young fellows just up and quit."

"Just like that?"

"Just like that."

"Any change with Joe?" Dorothea asked gently.

"Not yet. He's a strong lad though. Here he was coming in early to help with the baking *and* acting as sergeant for Chief Goodman. He'll pull through." He straightened his somewhat drooped shoulders. "Now what can I do for you?"

She told him of her bake sale plan and the need for a cookie recipe that could be unique for the Girl Guide troop. He said he'd give it some thought. She asked for a pan of cinnamon buns to be set aside for pick up after meeting with Mrs. Roberts and then took her leave. A dark-haired, bespectacled young man with the shadow of a moustache had stepped inside the shop and he held the door for her as she left.

Now, she thought, *on to Mrs. Roberts.*

At The Imperial she knocked at the door of the hotel's largest suite. The door was opened by a tall woman in a fashionable dress with geometric patterns whom Dorothea guessed to be in her early forties.

"Mrs. Roberts?" queried Dorothea. "I am Dorothea Montgomery."

"Delighted to make your acquaintance, Mrs. Montgomery and, yes, I am Mrs. Roberts—Frances

Roberts. Please come in. Let me take your coat. I'm envious of you that you've been outdoors already. I've been itching to go for a walk. The day looks splendid."

"It is indeed."

"My daughter Elspeth," said Mrs. Roberts, turning to the fresh-faced young woman who had followed her mother to the door.

Elspeth smiled shyly and held out a hand, her slender wrist clinking quietly with pearl bangles.

Further into the room, a man rose from an armchair with a book in his hand. He was square jawed with smoothly slicked backed hair and he too looked to be just into his forties. He strode over to her smiling and extending his hand for her handshake. "I'm Robert Roberts. Glad to meet you."

It suddenly occurred to Dorothea that her being here was, in fact, a little odd so she put herself into the role of the town's welcoming committee.

"On behalf of the townsfolk of Willowsdown, I hope you've been enjoying your stay so far," she began. "Are you here for long?" The little group had moved into the sitting area and Dorothea took a seat in the proffered chair.

"Just another day or so," Mrs. Roberts answered quickly. "We're heading to Toronto to hear concerts at Massey Hall then on to Niagara Falls and eventually New York City for the Metropolitan Opera. I adore opera." She glanced significantly at her husband who seemed to wince at the mention of opera.

"And you're from..?" asked Dorothea.

"Northern Minnesota," said Mr. Roberts.

"West of us then," said Dorothea more as a commentary to herself. They likely couldn't help her with her Vermont inquiries.

"A business trip for me, pleasure for the ladies. It's been a pleasure so far, hasn't it, Elspeth?"

Elspeth looked at her mother before replying, "Yes, Papa."

"Robert enjoys reading which can be done anywhere," said Frances Roberts.

"And you enjoy walking and listening to music which can also be done anywhere," responded Robert Roberts.

"Not everywhere, dearest," replied Frances coolly.

Elspeth was glancing back and forth between her parents during this exchange with what looked to Dorothea like a pained expression.

"And what do you enjoy, Elspeth?" asked Dorothea.

"Well," began Elspeth hesitantly, "I guess to some extent everything my parents like."

"And, of course, young men in military uniform," said Mrs. Roberts teasingly.

Elspeth blushed and smiled.

"But evidently he wasn't so keen," said Mr. Roberts bluntly. "Just as well. I couldn't have sanctioned it."

Mrs. Roberts had turned her back on her husband and Dorothea could almost see the hairs rising on her neck.

"Oh, are you referring to the young officer who was staying here recently?" Dorothea asked.

"Left abruptly. You must've scared him off, Elspeth," said Mr. Roberts.

"She did no such thing," bristled Mrs. Roberts. "This is a ridiculous conversation."

Dorothea decided that definitely these weren't the people who could help her with the paper about Vermont so she said smoothly, "I'm sorry you won't be here longer. We do have a Readers' Club to which you would be most welcome. Our town's band can't compete with anything at Massey Hall but they give a good concert come Victoria Day. There's also a delightful walk along the river. At this time of the year all the willow trees are freshly green. And there is an old apple orchard where the town's pie makers pick their apples in the fall. The only apples for pies are Northern Spies is the saying. Its trees will be budding. Nothing says hope like a fruit tree in bud."

"Wonderful!" exclaimed Mrs. Roberts energetically. "I've certainly been cooped up long enough today. I'm going to explore this walkway."

"Don't let me take up anymore of your time," said Dorothea, getting up from her chair. "I just wanted to be sure you were feeling welcome in Willowsdown."

Mr. Roberts stood also. "Not necessary but appreciated."

The Roberts family saw Dorothea to the door where Mr. Roberts helped her back into her coat. Pulling on her gloves, Dorothea said to him, "My husband, Charles, is starting up cricket practice next week so if you change your minds and decide to stay longer, you'd be welcome to the adventure that is cricket."

"Oh, Robert would rather read about it than actually play," laughed Mrs. Roberts mirthlessly.

Mr. Roberts regarded his wife remotely while holding the door for Dorothea.

It was Elspeth who said politely but sincerely, "Thank you for calling, Mrs. Montgomery."

Dorothea stood for a moment, blinking in the hotel hallway. She hadn't meant her visit to be so short but that was a decidedly unhappy family circle.

Back at North's Bakery she was surprised to see behind the counter, along with Ambrose North, the dark-haired, bespectacled young man who had entered the bakery as she had exited on her way to The Imperial.

"Ah, here you are. The cinnamon rolls will be ready in two shakes of a lamb's tail. Mrs. Montgomery, this is my hired-on-the-spot new employee Nat Thompson."

Nat had been kneading bread at the enamel-topped counter behind the front counter's display case.

"Don't let me interrupt your work, Nat. I'll just wave at you," said Dorothea with a twinkle. He had looked a little flummoxed as to what to do with his flour-covered hands.

"Think I have an idea for your Girl Guide cookies," continued Ambrose North. "I want to mull it over a bit more but I'll bring the recipe to the meeting tonight."

"That would be perfect. We need to get a move on with the baking to have enough to sell at the Victoria Day celebration."

"I'll be on it. Time and tide wait for no man. By the way, Nat," said Mr. North as he handed Dorothea her brown bag of cinnamon buns, "in case I'm not here, don't sell this last rhubarb pie. Alex Kaminen will be in just before closing. He always stops by for a piece of pie after making his meat order delivery at The Imperial. He leaves this evening for a week. Thought he might like the whole pie for his journey."

"Alex Kaminen; I'll remember," replied Nat.

"Lovely to meet you, Nat. You'll enjoy working at North's Bakery," said Dorothea encouragingly. "See you this evening, Ambrose."

"7:00 at The Imperial," he nodded.

Dorothea walked home, delivered the bag of cinnamon buns to Mrs. White, proudly pointing out that nary a one was missing which sometimes could unaccountably happen as she strolled home, and then spent what remained of the afternoon at her desk. Everyone attending this evening's Victoria Day planning meeting would eat a light supper because

Ambrose North invariably arrived with the day's leftover loaves of bread along with butter and jam. While she and Charles were eating, Dorothea tilted her head at Charles and asked,

"Do you know of any illegal stills in town?"

Charles choked slightly as he swallowed his devilled egg.

"Illegal stills? I see. You don't want me to get prescriptions from Dr. Payne anymore. You just want to go ahead and make you own. Is that right?"

Charles referred to the widely used practise of obtaining spirits for medical purposes.

"Prohibition is all but done, my dear," he continued. "Just hang onto your hat."

"Aren't you a card. No. I was just wondering if Joe's accident could have anything to do with some kind of alcohol sales? What with everything that goes on just down the road so to speak in Waterloo."

"Mmmm, maybe. It's worth bringing it up with the chief."

"That's what I thought. So … do you know of any illegal activity?"

He tilted his head to match hers.

"I really couldn't say."

Dorothea and Charles meandered to the meeting savouring the smell of spring and the lingering light that betokened longer days. Robins parasailed across the street, chuckling and chirruping. Doves could be heard cooing under bushes. A cardinal, a spot of crimson perched atop a towering jack pine, raised his anthem to the twilight. Dorothea remarked to Charles how different this evening was to the previous evening when she and the Wainfleets had found Joe North lying beside the railway track. Nearing The Imperial, they noted a knot of townspeople gathered on the sidewalk in front of the main entrance. Mrs. Johnson broke away from the group and swept toward the Montgomerys wringing her hands.

"Oh! Mrs. Montgomery! Mr. Montgomery! It's monstrous! Shocking! Tragic!"

Dorothea was fond of the ebullient Mrs. Johnson but because Mrs. Johnson loved to wrap her tongue around the most expressive words she could think of regardless of their aptness, Dorothea was wont to take her statements with a grain of salt. She imagined that this monstrous tragedy had something to do with an absent agenda or a reneged responsibility. She smiled and asked, "What is tragic, Mrs. Johnson?"

"Well! Well! The American visitor Mr. Roberts has been found dead! Murdered it would seem!"

Chapter Three

Dorothea and Charles were struck dumb. Charles had winked at Dorothea as Mrs. Johnson approached them with her wringing hands and tale of woe but now he wished he could take it back.

"Mr. Roberts," repeated Dorothea somewhat stupidly.

"Yes! My presumption is that his wife did it."

Dorothea looked past Mrs. Johnson at the group of townspeople who were talking animatedly with Charles who had now joined them. She took Mrs. Johnson's arm and, walking towards the clump of people, she said quietly, "I'm sure your kind heart and understanding of justice will keep you from casting aspersions on anyone. We wouldn't want to do anything to muddle up the case for Chief Goodman or cause harm to anyone's character."

"Of course, Mrs. Montgomery, of course," she paused. "'Aspersions'! My, my, that's a useful word… but between you and me, I must say this. Whenever Mr. and Mrs. Roberts procured goods at the Emporium, many sour looks did she toss his way."

If it wasn't such a somber subject, Dorothea would have laughed—the tossing of sour looks does not a murderer make she wanted to point out; instead she said, "we can all be annoyed with someone we love."

"Yes, but others in town also have taken heed of the acrimony between them."

"Nonetheless, Mrs. Johnson," she said firmly.

Nelson Goodman Jr. was nudging his way through the crowd. Nelson Jr. was Chief Goodman's eldest son.

Last summer he had announced his intention of following his father into police work and had applied himself diligently since then to any task assigned to him. He came up to Dorothea and Mrs. Johnson.

"Mrs. Montgomery, Dad, ah, Chief Goodman would be obliged if we could put your "noticing" skills to work."

"Certainly," replied Dorothea. She nodded at Mrs. Johnson and then she and Nelson Jr. strode through the opening in the cluster of townsfolk and stepped into the hotel's foyer.

"I'll tell you what we know so far," began Nelson Jr., removing his cap as they headed towards the stairs, "which as Dad says is bloody little. Mr. Roberts was found by his wife at the bottom of the spiral staircase in their suite. They're in the suite that covers two stories."

Dorothea nodded. "Yes, I visited them this afternoon."

"You did? What for?" he asked.

Dorothea hesitated. The papers about Vermont couldn't have anything to do with Mr. Roberts' death. To disclose their existence now would just muddy the waters and delay solving the mystery of what did happen to him.

Her head tipped sideways as she answered, "I thought I'd make sure they were feeling welcome in town and enjoying their stay."

"Ah. Well, his wife, Frances Roberts, found him. That was a bit before 6:00 p.m. She was returning from a walk. She says her daughter, Elspeth, came in after. Miss Roberts said she had been at the library. Dad ... the chief, is talking with them right now and Dr. Payne is examining Mr. Roberts' body. I've begun taking fingerprints."

For the second time that day, Dorothea found herself in The Imperial's most splendid suite. The door opened onto a tiled entryway with a closet to the left and a hat stand and hallway table on the right with a mirror over the table. The tile ended and one stepped onto the plush white carpet of a large sitting room. To the right was an electric fireplace surrounded by a neatly carved mantelpiece and the whole area, scattered about with chairs, a couch and a loveseat also in white, was presided over by three floor to ceiling windows. During the day, light tumbled in with happy profusion but now it was the grey sighs of the twilight that seeped into the space. Across the room from the electric fire and mantelpiece was the spiral staircase that led upstairs to two bedrooms and a study. There at the bottom of the staircase lay the crumpled body of Mr. Roberts. Dr. Payne, just finalizing his preliminary examination, was leaning over the body.

Dr. Payne nodded his head at Dorothea. "Good evening, Mrs. Montgomery. Sad business. Your Dad was right, Junior: a broken neck."

Dorothea looked down at Mr. Roberts' body. The head, with the face upturned at an unnatural angle to the torso, was on the floor and the legs were draped up the last few steps.

"Is that a bruise on his left cheek, Dr. Payne, or 5:00 shadow?"

"Good eye, Mrs. Montgomery. It's a bruise but a very slight one. A nasty contusion here on the right temple but it's clean. A cut high up on the right temple also clean but dried blood a bit further back on his scalp. Also some dried blood in his nose."

"Result of a nose bleed?" asked Dorothea.

"Maybe. Except his nose was broken," replied the doctor.

"Couldn't that be from the fall?" Dorothea queried.

"It could," the doctor agreed.

"But there should be blood if he had cut his head during his fall, shouldn't there?"

"Indeed. Junior, tell your dad the body of Mr. Roberts can be removed. I'll call Arthur at the funeral home and tell him to come as quickly as possible so the ladies needn't be trapped upstairs much longer. I'll do further examinations there."

"Right, Dr. Payne."

Nelson Jr. stepped around the body to mount the stairs to where Chief Goodman was interviewing the Roberts women. Dr. Payne packed up his bag. Dorothea wandered to the sitting area. She stood between the couch and the coffee table looking towards the mantelpiece.

Dorothea noticed what had the look of grease marks on the wall to the left of the mantelpiece. She stepped over to touch them. There were three spots in a diagonal line to each other all about three inches long. It wasn't grease that had marked the wall though. The marks all felt slightly wet. She scrutinized the carpet. There too were smudged spots. They had a pale rusty look to them and were also damp. Turning slowly in a circle she scanned the area around the mantelpiece. There didn't seem to be any further marks to mar the whiteness of the carpet or couch and chairs. She stepped carefully towards the staircase, this time closely examining the carpet. She skirted Dr. Payne and the body of Mr. Roberts and on the fourth step from the bottom of the staircase Dorothea noticed a shadowy smudge on the white carpet. She touched the spot. It was damp. She began a slow ascent scanning the remaining steps. At the curve in the spiral, another step showed a shadowy smudge also slightly damp. The staircase was metal with the white carpet wrapped around each of the steps and on the metal railing at even intervals, were bronze coronets which if a person were to hit their head against one would certainly cause an impressive abrasion and a denting of the skull. At the top of the staircase she met the Goodmans.

"Mrs. Montgomery," said Chief Goodman softly. "Thank you for coming. Mrs. Roberts and Miss Roberts are lying down on their beds. Junior, finish the fingerprints for downstairs and get them to the station."

"Right, Dad ... Chief."

Down the hall to the left of the staircase were two bedrooms and to the right, a bathroom and a study. Dorothea peeked into the bathroom as she passed. On the shower curtain rack hung a dress. Dorothea could see that one of the cuffs was damp. Over the rim of the tub a man's initialed handkerchief was smoothly laid out. She could distinguish that it too was not dry and showed some pale stains. Beside where she stood in the doorway was a white wicker laundry hamper. She lifted the lid: a few large towels and one very wet and dully stained hand towel. Other than that, all in the white and black tiled bathroom seemed entirely in order. From there she moved to the study. Standing inside its threshold she surveyed the room slowly. The walls were painted a blue grey, the first non-white room she had seen so far. To her left under a window was a large desk covered with piles of correspondence held down with various paperweights and a phone with a pewter base. On the wall across from where she stood was an oak mantelpiece framing another electric fireplace. To her right was a small sitting area backed by shelves where presumably guests could place books or any other paraphernalia to make their stay pleasant. In keeping with Frances Roberts' claim that her husband preferred reading to many other activities, the shelves were lined with books. A Persian carpet with a tree of life motif of grey and gold hues almost covered the hardwood floor. She walked over to the desk.

"We'll be gathering up his correspondence and whatever else is here and taking it to the station," stated Chief Goodman.

"Does it look to you like any of the paper weights were used against Mr. Roberts?"

"Too early to tell."

"Did you notice the smudges on the wall and carpet in the sitting area downstairs or on the steps?"

Chief Goodman rubbed his bald head. "Can't say that I did."

She thought of the rusty stained towel in the laundry hamper. "I think," she began slowly, "that someone has been cleaning. There is a wet and stained towel in the hamper."

The chief nodded his head. "Yep, I did notice that."

"I think those are blood stains on that towel."

Chief Goodman blew air between his teeth. He never had learned to whistle. "So maybe not accidental then."

"Maybe not."

They both began studying the walls and floor and carpet of the study.

"Doesn't seem to be anything here," the chief eventually said. "I'd like to see what you saw downstairs."

As they descended the staircase, Dorothea pointed out the smudge marks she had previously seen.

"These look the same as the spots that I'll show you in the living area; as though blood has been cleaned away."

"Hmmm—I see."

At the bottom of the steps, Dr. Payne had moved Mr. Roberts' body aside and covered it with his overcoat.

In the sitting area, Dorothea pointed out the marks on the wall and carpet.

"You're right," said the chief after touching the spots. "They're damp. And they do have the look of someone trying to scrub out blood stains."

Dorothea asked, "What did the Roberts women say?"

He indicated to the chairs and they both sat.

"Mrs. Roberts claimed she had been walking for over an hour. Prior to that, she had taken tea in the dining room downstairs."

"Others would have seen her then. Did anyone see her during her walk?"

"She says so but she can't say who they were since she knows so few people in town."

"And Elspeth?"

"She says she was at the library."

"Easy enough to confirm."

"Yes."

There was a soft knock on the door and it opened.

"Ah, Arthur. Glad to see you," said Chief Goodman.

Dorothea and the town's young funeral director exchanged greetings and Dorothea asked Chief Goodman, "Do you mind if I stay for a few minutes? I would like to tap on Mrs. Robert's door."

"By all means."

At the top of the stairs, Dorothea contemplated the two closed doors and realized she didn't know which one to tap on to reference Mrs. Roberts. While she was standing there the door to her left opened. Mrs. Roberts looked at her—defiantly it seemed to Dorothea and from a markedly untearstained face.

"Mrs. Roberts, I'm so sorry for your loss."

"My loss," repeated Frances Roberts dully.

"May I make you a cup of tea?"

"Not tea, no. Prohibition! What I want is brandy."

"It's possible there's a bottle hidden in the hotel's restaurant. Shall I make discreet inquiries?" asked Dorothea, tilting her head.

Mrs. Roberts raised her eyebrows and nodded.

"Arthur Poole from the funeral home is downstairs. Would you like me to bring what I find to the study?"

"No, not the study. Downstairs is fine. I'm sure they won't be long," she said, moving toward the staircase.

Peering over the railing, Dorothea could see that Arthur Poole had tightly wrapped Mr. Roberts' body in a blanket. He and Nelson Jr. were transferring it to a stretcher and Dr. Payne was shrugging on his coat. Mrs. Roberts paused in her descent and watched the men carry the stretcher to the door. At the door, they put it down, slipped their galoshes on, opened the door and proceeded outside. Chief Goodman followed them out and gently closed the door behind him. Mrs. Roberts had been right; they hadn't been long about it. Descending the stairs, again, she and Frances Roberts parted ways at the bottom: Frances to a white chair beside the long windows and Dorothea to her quest for forbidden liquor.

"I checked on Elspeth. She seems to have fallen asleep," said Frances. The large diamond in her engagement ring flashed under the light of the chandelier as she reached for the glass Dorothea held out to her. "Please sit down."

Dorothea lowered herself onto a white chair in the sitting room. She glanced around her, nonchalantly she hoped, looking for anything that appeared different from when she and Chief Goodman had inspected the area earlier. It had taken some time to convince Mr. Schlessinger, the hotel manager, to admit that he had the bottle that Dorothea knew he had and in that time it was possible that if Mrs. Roberts had something to hide she could easily have done so. Nothing was apparently any different.

They sat in silence while Mrs. Roberts eagerly gulped down some of the brandy. "I didn't love my husband," said Mrs. Roberts bluntly.

Heavens, thought Dorothea. *What was in that glass?*

"Not anymore at any rate," continued Mrs. Roberts. "When we first met, oh 20 odd years ago, I adored him. He was articulate and fearless; obviously primed for success in business; he seemed to truly listen to me when I talked; and we talked a lot. He was extremely well read—so different than many of the men I knew growing up. But then as life continued it became apparent that if he had loved me, his business interests had usurped my place in his heart. Whatever he set his hand to prospered—and consumed him. He was attentive to Elspeth when she was a little girl but as she moved towards womanhood he seemed to peer at her as at a speculative business opportunity. Who would be rich enough to buy shares in his daughter?"

Mrs. Roberts glared at Dorothea daring her to balk at such a statement.

"And how did Elspeth feel towards her father?"

"Well, naturally she loved him," replied Mrs. Roberts and took another hefty gulp from her glass.

"Why naturally?"

"She remembered the early days and kept looking for their return."

"Is there someone Mr. Roberts considered, 'rich enough to buy shares in his daughter'?"

"Not that I know of. There was recently someone he certainly considered as not rich enough."

"And that was…?"

Mrs. Roberts abruptly set down her glass and rose from her seat.

"Mrs. Montgomery, I thank you for your efforts on my behalf," she nodded at the glass, "but I feel the need to be alone."

"Of course. You have my card so please call on me if there is anything you need."

So, thought Dorothea as she walked home, *either the woman is entirely innocent or she's calling a bluff.* Come to think of it, Mrs. Roberts doesn't even know that Chief Goodman suspects foul play. If she killed her husband she's assuming it was so cleverly done as to be above suspicion and thus the frank heart to heart. Time would tell as to whether or not Elspeth would be as forthcoming. Passing North's Bakery, which even now gave off a whiff of yeasty yumminess, Dorothea saw an upright figure standing on the doorstep as if uncertain as to what to do. It was Nat Thompson, Mr. North's new employee.

"Hello, Nat, you're looking as though you're unsure of where to go," Dorothea teased gently. A thought struck her. "You do have a place to stay?"

"Oh, yes," Nat replied, coming out of his reverie and standing up even straighter if that was possible. "I have a room at The Imperial until I find something more permanent."

"They're a bit at sixes and sevens over there with the tragedy of Mr. Roberts' death. He was a visitor from the States. His wife and daughter are still there."

"I had heard something about it," he said, pulling the cuffs down on his jacket. "Well, I should go. I have an early start. Good evening."

"Yes, good evening, Nat."

When Dorothea turned her head to look down the street as she crossed, Nat was still standing on the same spot looking toward The Imperial.

Chapter Four

Dorothea awoke the next morning to the terrible thought that someone in her town had deliberately taken the life of another created being. From the adjoining bathroom she could hear Charles tapping his shaving brush on the side of his lathering bowl. She tossed her pillow onto the floor, laid herself flat on her back with arms tight to her sides and pointed her toes. This was her thinking position while lying in bed. Ever since childhood it had yielded good results.

"Dorothea? Are you awake?"

She could tell by the sound of his voice that while delicately shaving around his Douglas Fairbanks moustache, Charles had again got soap in his mouth.

"Yes. I'm thinking."

Running water, spitting, tapping of razor and brush against the sink.

"Good, because apparently Chief Goodman was here early this morning to bring you up to date. He left a note with Betty and Dilman."

She knew that she had no official capacity to be included in any kind of investigation so she deeply appreciated Chief Goodman's trust in her discretion and what he termed her "noticing abilities". Those abilities were mostly put to use in the day to day interactions of people just doing life together. A tone of voice or movement of an eyebrow or a new piece of clothing may point to an emotional situation that needs attention. She remembered this past autumn when she noticed a neighbour was not wearing her wedding ring. Apparently she had taken it off a week previously and no one in her family—parents, siblings—all who lived nearby, had noticed. Dorothea happened to stop by while the woman was raking leaves in her yard and as they chatted she took in the glaring omission and gently asked if something was wrong. From there, an entire story of unhappiness and misunderstanding came tumbling out. There is no easy way ahead in a rocky marriage but if both are willing to climb over boulders together a new path can be formed. Dorothea hadn't spoken with the woman for several months but a few weeks ago she had waved at Dorothea as she cycled past and Dorothea saw the flash of gold on her left hand.

A modest ability, Dorothea admitted and yet one that could be put to use in diverse scenarios. Like the one facing Chief Goodman and the folk of Willowsdown.

In the kitchen about 20 minutes later, Mrs. White handed Dorothea the note.

"Did he say anything else?"

"No. Just that he had moved the Roberts women to another suite and he wanted you to stop by the police station and look at the fingerprints Nelson Jr. got and to look at the photos taken," answered Betty, holding aloft the coffee pot.

"Yes. Thank you, Betty."

"Don't see why Nelson needs someone else poking about," mumbled a voice behind a newspaper. The translation of this was: she, Dorothea, might be put to unnecessary strain and even danger where he, Dilman White, could not protect her.

A number of years back Dilman had been involved with the police—something to do with the then new Prohibition laws. Charles had spoken on Dilman's behalf. Dorothea had never heard one way or the other about Dilman's guilt or innocence but since then the

Montgomerys had an unswervingly loyal employee if a bit of an outspoken one.

"Don't be daft, man," exclaimed Betty White. "Joe usually helps Nelson and he's down injured so someone needs to help find out what happened. It's likely nothing at all. Some neighbourhood prank and Joe just tripped on the railway line. Easy as anything to do in the dusk. Mark my words."

"That's all fine," retorted Dilman. "But what about this foreigner getting himself killed here in our town? Them Yankees. You never know what sort of shoot-up they bring with them."

"He wasn't shot, Dilman," said Dorothea.

"Hmph," said the voice behind the paper.

Dorothea read the chief's note. "Moved the Roberts ladies into another suite. Junior took photographs of all the rooms and did fingerprinting. Would like you to cast your eye over all." She wasn't sure why he bothered with a note since he must know it would be read; he might just as well have told Mrs. White. She knew the sterling character of the Whites, and of Dianna, and that no one in their employ would ever read anything of official or real importance but when it came to notes from townspeople…. Mrs. White seemed to have put herself in the role of the wine taster to the king as in days of old. Rather than poisoned wine she would be sure that no poisoned pen reached Dorothea.

"You wouldn't want someone unjustly accused of something they didn't do would you, Dilman?" asked Dorothea just a little archly.

The paper rustled. "'Course not."

"Well, with Joe not available, we need all hands on deck."

"Anyway, husband of mine, Mrs. Montgomery is good at this sort of thing and doesn't need a bodyguard. You're best to be out in the garden."

No answer.

"I'm going to start asking questions at the library. I think we can count on that being a safe enough place," said Dorothea finishing her coffee. She flicked the newspaper as she left the kitchen and heard a snort of laughter.

As she told Betty and Dilman, she had already decided that after looking over Chief Goodman's information, she would head to the library to confirm Elspeth had been there. She was sure she had been because there seemed no reason at all for Elspeth to cause her father harm. Daughters simply did not kill their fathers because he didn't approve her heart's choice. Girls were much more resilient than that.

When Dorothea stepped into the police station with its checkerboard floor, the chief and his son were standing at the counter poring over the photographs. A portrait of King George V and the May cow on the local creamery's calendar looked mildly down on them.

"Mrs. Montgomery, thanks for coming. We've kept the Roberts' suite as it was but thought photos would be good backup. Miss Roberts wanted the dress that was hanging in the bathroom and the handkerchief. She said it was the handkerchief her father always used for his nosebleeds. Don't think I'd keep something like that for sentimental reasons but then everyone's different. I'm wondering about it a bit though since we found a handkerchief in his pants' pocket and it was bloodstained."

"He might have needed two handkerchiefs for a nosebleed," commented Dorothea.

"Maybe. We haven't accounted for all the fingerprints. A print on the mantelpiece needs an owner," said Nelson Jr.

"Did you confirm the stains on the towel?" asked Dorothea.

"Yep and they're blood," stated the chief.

"The handkerchiefs weren't enough for a nose bleed and the towel was used?" queried Dorothea.

"Maybe," nodded the chief.

"But it still doesn't explain the wet spots on the wall and carpet," mused Dorothea.

"He could have dripped blood on the carpet before getting a hold of his handkerchief or the towel," said Nelson Jr.

Dorothea had been vaguely shuffling through the photos but stopped and picked up one showcasing the handkerchief on the tub rim.

"Didn't you say that Elspeth wanted this handkerchief for sentimental reasons?"

Father and son peered at the photo. "Yep." They both nodded.

"Because it was her father's?"

"Yep." Both nodded again.

"Look at the initials."

"T.N.," they said in unison.

"T.N.?" repeated Nelson Jr. "Who's T.N.?"

"Well, either Miss Elspeth got her handkerchiefs mixed up or she's hiding something," said Chief Goodman grimly.

"Shall I talk to her?" asked Dorothea.

"It's worth a shot," agreed the chief. "I can always come along later as the heavy hand of the law."

"I'll start by asking questions at the library," offered Dorothea.

"Good idea. Junior and I are going to try and figure out who was out walking at the same time as Mrs. Roberts." He sighed. "I sure could use Joe North right about now. Half the town could've been out walking for all I know."

Dorothea patted his arm encouragingly. "Get Edwina to help you. She'll narrow down who was supposed to be where and when and so who might be out for a stroll."

Chief Goodman brightened. "You're right. Junior get a hold of Mrs. Quayle."

"Right you are, Chief."

"I'll report back sometime later?"

"That'd be great, Mrs. Montgomery. Dr. Payne should have his autopsy report by then."

At the library, Dorothea discovered that Elspeth had certainly been there. Miss Kalbfleisch, the librarian, distinctly remembered Elspeth's arrival because Elspeth had managed to knock most the books off the trolley that was destined to return them to their shelves.

"She was mortified, poor thing. She has come to the library a few times and although she's quiet, she seemed to me to be a warm-hearted girl. Very pleasant and approachable," said Miss Kalbfleisch.

"I met her briefly yesterday but my impression was similar to yours. I'm sure you've heard about the death of Robert Roberts, Elspeth's father."

"Yes. Very sad. And so far from home."

"Indeed. Did Elspeth stay long here at the library?"

Miss Kalbfleisch and Dorothea had known one another for many years now. She was well aware of Dorothea's reputation as a "noticer" and not a busybody noticer but a discerning noticer. She peered at Dorothea keenly. Dorothea returned the gaze serenely.

"Of that I can't be certain. She passed by the desk here, turning right which leads to the front door. But ... she may have gone upstairs to the junior library. She didn't meet my eyes as she passed. I assumed that she was still embarrassed by the upset of the books. But you know, as I think about it, she actually seemed agitated. More than knocking over some books would account for. Anyway, at the time I really thought nothing of it and once she passed the desk, I gave her no further thought; besides another patron needed a book signed out so I didn't clearly take note of her movements." She paused. "Should I have?" she asked with arched brows.

Dorothea tilted her head. "Perhaps. But then, 'discretion in the interval…'"

"Emily Dickinson," nodded Miss Kabfleisch.

"Just so. But you remember when Elspeth arrived because of the book upset."

"Yes. I had finished my tea in the staff room and was returning to the desk so that would have been around 4:20 p.m."

"Thank you, Miss Kalbfleisch. I'll go chat with Miss Weber in the junior library."

Upstairs, Miss Weber confirmed that Elspeth had been in the junior library but that she spent her time sitting by one of the windows looking over the main street. Miss Weber said that as it seemed Miss Roberts wasn't needing immediate attention, she took herself to the back room for a few minutes to catalogue some of the more dated library books. When she returned into the main area, Miss Roberts had gone.

"Would you have any idea what time that might have been?" asked Dorothea.

Miss Weber shifted the pile of books crooked in her left arm to her right. "Umm, well, I don't think I could say for sure…. I really wasn't watching the clock."

"I see." Dorothea realized that since she really had no official right to be asking who, what, why, when, where, how questions she was at a loss as to how else to get helpful information. Mr. Roberts was dead but Chief Goodman had not confirmed foul play. It could be pointed out that officially it was none of her business. And she certainly couldn't keep this up because there were mothers and children beginning to ascend the stairs for the morning's story time.

"Has the most recent 'Just William' book been returned? My grandchildren like to read the William books when they come to visit."

"Not yet, Mrs. Montgomery."

"I'll check on it again another time then. Thank you, Miss Weber."

Dorothea made her way down the opposite side of the stairs from the straggling clumps of mothers and children nodding and greeting as she went.

Miss Weber stood at the top of the stairs smiling at her patrons but with an eye on Dorothea and the front door. When Dorothea was clearly outside on the steps chatting with another mother, Miss Weber nipped into the back room where the phone sat on a table in a corner. With the few moments she had while everyone settled, she lifted the receiver, was connected to the phone exchange and told her tale, such as it was, into the ear of the operator who would most want to know.

Chief Goodman waited patiently while Nat Thompson carefully sliced several loaves of bread for the customer ahead of him. He vaguely remembered hearing that somewhere in the United States someone had come up with a machine that would do the job instead. Why on earth anyone would need to have a machine that sliced one's bread was beyond his comprehension. Surely it didn't take up that much time in a day to slice bread. And besides if you sliced your own as needed it could be as thin or thick as desired. Were people getting lazier or just more monotonous? Presumably the lady in front of him did not have time to slice bread because she was standing and waiting for someone else to do it for her. He could hear in the back room the rhythmic drone of the standing mixer that he knew was turning over cookie dough. He knew this because his oldest daughter was running the mixer. From earliest years she had loved to help her mother bake. Chief Goodman's wife, who was frequently unwell, would have been happy to retain this help in the home kitchen but she was also a prudent woman. "Why not get paid for doing something you love?" she had asked their daughter. Somehow although in-the-home baking was the woman's realm, out in the working world it was the realm of men. Nevertheless, Ambrose North had been willing to hire Miss Goodman on trial. Although tongues had wagged at the time, he hadn't regretted his decision. "Worth her weight in salt," he'd told the Chief which, of course, caused some chest puffing on his part.

"…doughnuts?"

Rising out of his reverie, he realized that the bread slicing had been accomplished and the customer on her way past him had been asking whether he had come in for doughnuts. He was rather known for his penchant for the bakery's honey glazed doughnuts.

"Yes, sorry, right you are. Definitely here for doughnuts," he vaguely replied raising his cap. Stepping to the counter, he said, "I'm Chief Goodman. I believe you're Nat Thompson?"

Nat dropped the knife he had been holding. Stooping to pick it up, he came up flushed.

"My daughter Nellie works here," explained Chief Goodman.

Nat slowly turned his head towards the kitchen and then back, nodding comprehendingly. He replaced the knife on the cutting board saying, "I've always been a bit clumsy and absent minded." Breathing deep, he smiled warmly. "Did I hear you say doughnuts?"

"Just a half dozen, please. Have you been in the bakery business long?" the chief asked making polite conversation.

"Ah … well, not long really. Well, that is to say not long in the business side of things. But some considerable time in the practice of it."

"I see. Any specialties?"

Nat reddened. "Cakes actually. Wedding cakes in particular."

"You don't say. Well. That's an important task. Found a place to live?"

"Not yet. I'm staying temporarily at The Imperial."

Chief Goodman stiffened into his professional role. "The Imperial. When did you check in there?"

"Yesterday morning."

"Thursday."

"Yes, sir."

"The morning of Roberts' death," muttered the Chief to himself.

"Your doughnuts, Chief Goodman," said Nat, handing the paper bag over the counter.

"Right. Thank you," replied the Chief, jingling the change in his pocket and counting out the needed amount.

At the police station, Chief Goodman sat munching a doughnut in his office and reading the autopsy report. Dr. Payne had written it in official medical terms and then on another sheet of paper translated it into layman's language which stated that Mr. Roberts had not died from the blow to the side of his head but from a broken neck. The contusion on the side of the head was on top of a deeply bruised area. Dr. Payne outlined his opinion that the bruising had been caused by something bluntly pointed as the bruised area was small though deep and the impact was enough to break skin causing at least a trickling of blood. The nose was broken from an impact on the left side. He stated the nose could have been broken during the fall which caused the broken neck. As his body was still warm, death had to have been not long before the body was found. Certainly within the hour.

Chief Goodman sighed. He supposed it could be accidental death but there was just too much blood and too many blows to allow him to leave it there. There was no one in town who knew Mr. Roberts. He and his wife and daughter were American strangers passing through. To him it seemed logical that either the wife or the daughter had killed him by pushing him down the stairs. And that was the line of inquiry he would take.

Chapter Five

Upon leaving the library, Dorothea took herself to The Imperial in search of Elspeth who, as it turned out, was not to be found. She decided to stop in at Charles' office at the insurance company and ask for details about Wednesday's chat with George. Willowsdown was not a large town so the impressive insurance building in its downtown was rather a source of civic pride. It had been built 15 years ago in 1912 replacing a much smaller building when Charles and his business partner realized that the growth in the insurance industry was not likely to slow down. It was sturdily and beautifully built in the Modern Renaissance style, constructed with light-brown and yellow, narrow Roman brick with a leaf and floral design under the cornice as well as over the many windows with warm oak doors reaching up 25 feet. Somehow its imposing structure didn't cause a quaking in the boots but just a sense of assurance. Suitable, considering it housed an assurance company.

Charles' office was on the second floor. Dorothea climbed the wide oak staircase and tried to appear as though she were not out of breath when she reached the top. *Twelve foot ceilings are all very well,* she thought *but they definitely add to the length of staircases.* Charles was not only in the office but unengaged. In fact, he was dunking one of Mrs. White's ginger cookies into a mug of tea.

"I certainly hope Mrs. White never retires from being our cook," began Charles. "How would I get through a morning without one of her ginger cookies?"

"I can make them you know, Charles," said Dorothea tilting her head.

"I know."

"Hmmm. Not as well apparently." After 36 years of marriage there aren't too many voice inflections that can't be interpreted.

"You do other things eminently well." Charles rose from his chair and coming around his desk kissed her forehead and pulled another chair from the front of the desk to stand beside his.

"I know," replied Dorothea buoyantly. "So, tell me about George." She settled into the chair, removed her gloves, unbuttoned her coat and reached for the last cookie.

"He is completely smitten with Elva. But I don't know....She's a new world girl and he's an old world boy. I had never really thought about the—how can I put it?—the cultural differences between here and there."

"Hmm," Dorothea mumbled through her cookie. "Maybe it's less—how shall I put it?—geographical and more experiential? George has never *had* to work or really even thought about what work he would do. Elva *has* to work in order to be independent. Thankfully, he is willing to work. He's shown promise here at the office, hasn't he?"

"Yes, no doubt about that. If he had simply decided to live on what he has and what he has coming to him I don't see how he and Elva could make themselves compatible. She needs someone to match her ambition and abilities."

"Charles! I believe you've hit the nail on the head! Is that what you said to him?"

"No. Just thought of it now. Not even sure where that came from."

"What *did* you say?"

"Not much of anything I rather think. I believe George just needed an ear. He pretty much repeated his bewilderment in various ways. Although he did say one thing that might indicate that he has an inkling into Elva's mind."

"Yes?"

"Something about her logical reasoning that had shown itself at book club meetings. It was that that had first drawn him to her. He said that maybe that would be dulled if she didn't have the energizing of a job from home. He was really muttering to himself at the time as though he were testing out the thought so my guess is that it's only a kernel in his understanding right now."

"Well, that's exactly the kernel that needs to be coaxed out! I think your insight just now may be the understanding he needs. I'm sure Elva just wants to know he's willing to budge in his fixed thinking. He's never needed to question or adapt it before now. It's even possible she won't necessarily stay working just so long as she knows he's not a dig-his-heels-in kind of a fellow; that it's not the job itself that's at issue but a, a what? A high-handedness, I think, would be the term, that she's seen in him. He's likely not even aware of it."

"Hmm, could be. I'll be seeing him tomorrow. He's helping me at the cricket pavilion organize the bats and wickets and so on. I'll try and bring the conversation around."

"My guess is that it won't take much. He really is heartbroken about the wedding being called off."

"What did Chief Goodman want?"

"He had some photographs for me to study. One of them was of a handkerchief that apparently Elspeth

Roberts said she wanted as a keepsake of her father. And yet the initials were T.N."

"T.N.? Odd. Did Roberts have another name? Or had that been a handkerchief that belonged to someone special to him?"

"Maybe. I confirmed that Elspeth had been to the library yesterday but for how long I don't know. Chief Goodman is waiting for the autopsy report. Which, come to think of it, he likely has by now. Were you still wanting me to check in with George Flesherton about wild turkeys?"

"Certainly. I can't go out hunting them myself but I do love a wild turkey dinner. If any of the local hunters bagged too many they'll take them to George."

"All right," said Dorothea, gathering her purse and gloves. "I'll stop at the police station and then head to the butcher shop." She blew him a kiss as she made her exit.

Chief Goodman was still mulling over the autopsy report when Dorothea stepped into the station. He stood up and motioned for her to take a seat in front of his desk.

"I've got it here. I'd like to land on accidental death but ...." He shrugged his shoulders and outlined to her about the broken neck and the bluntly pointed object causing the bruising and abrasion on the right side of the head. About the nose being broken from the left side.

"My money is on the wife or daughter," he said.

"I don't understand how it is that there is evidence of blood downstairs and yet he was found at the bottom of the staircase. If there had been a coming to blows before pushing him downstairs wouldn't that have been in evidence upstairs?" asked Dorothea.

"There's the possibility that the blow to the head and the broken nose happened on the way down the stairs. Those coronets on the railing would do a number on any head or nose. But it still begs the question of the blood in the living area," commented Chief Goodman.

"Knowing how it was done would help us to know who did it I should think. And yet who did it could also narrow down the how. A broken nose seems to indicate some kind of force which doesn't quite match with Mrs. Roberts or Elspeth. Particularly not Elspeth."

"In Elspeth's case I could see the coronets theory adding up. Mrs. Roberts seems to me a more aggressive type; she might've lashed out physically at her husband."

"Punched him in the nose, do you think?"

"Possibly."

"And she really was in the dining room having tea in the afternoon?"

"Definitely. Not only that, but Mr. Roberts was there briefly along with Elspeth."

"Elspeth? So, she was there before going to the library."

"Let me take a look here at Junior's notes. Right. It says that Mrs. Roberts and Elspeth were in the hotel dining room by about 4:00 p.m. They ordered only a pot of coffee which they were drinking when Mr. Roberts joined them at about 10 minutes after 4:00 p.m. Mr. Schlessinger stated that he felt tension amongst them. In fact, it seemed to him that Mr. Roberts had possibly been drinking. At some point Elspeth left. He didn't see her leave. Mr. and Mrs. Roberts continued at the table. By 4:30 p.m. only Mrs. Roberts was still at the table. After that he can't account for her movements because he was busy in the kitchen. Alex Kaminen had delivered the meat order from George Flesherton's shop and since he would be away for a week and someone else would be doing the order for him next week, he and Mr. Schlessinger were instructing the young fellow on what went where and so on."

"But there would have been other people in the dining room as well as the wait staff. Surely they can tell us something."

"Yep, just gettin' to that. The young woman serving the Roberts said that Mrs. Roberts was gone from the table likely by 4:40 p.m. She too admitted that the Roberts didn't seem happy with each other. There were three women seated two tables from the Roberts. They were trying not to hear the conversation but they did hear Mrs. Roberts say, 'I'm done with this and I'm going to stop you. I don't know how but I will.'"

"Oh."

"They couldn't hear what Mr. Roberts said but he laughed. They noticed that he carried a glass with him as he left the table and they also stated they thought he seemed tipsy."

"Did the waitress remember when Elspeth left?"

"She says that Elspeth didn't stay long after Mr. Roberts joined them. Maybe 10 minutes. She noticed that Elspeth was crying as she left."

"That glass. Did he have it when he arrived at the table or had he ordered something?"

"Not sure."

"Here's another thought. If Mr. Roberts had been drinking perhaps he fell down the stairs on his own."

"Maybe. We didn't see any alcohol in the suite but it's worth a look. Several people, when interviewed separately, remarked on his drunk, or at least somewhat drunken, state."

"Especially if the glass came with him into the dining room."

"Right."

"All this does make us sure of one thing though and that is that Mr. Roberts was still alive at 4:30 p.m. Did Mrs. Roberts go to the suite before her walk and kill him? Did Elspeth slip out of the library and kill him after her mother left for a walk? Come to think of it, Miss Weber said that Elspeth was sitting in one of the window sills that looks out over Main Street which would clearly give her a view of The Imperial and her mother's departure for her walk. But there's absolutely nothing of conclusive evidence to put Elspeth in the role of murderess. Or for that matter Mrs. Roberts, except for her forthright personality and that overheard comment. Are we making a mountain out of a mole hill?"

"There were signs of violence on Mr. Roberts and in the room. Something happened that was not accidental."

"Yes," sighed Dorothea. "You're right."

"Junior and I'll search the suite again. I'll let you know what we find."

Chief Goodman poured himself a coffee after Dorothea left. A pot was left warming on the potbellied stove the livelong day and by the end of the day it tasted rather like tar. At this time of the day, though, it was more like molasses so mostly drinkable. He knew that in official police circles to include a civilian in an investigation was not done—and for good reason. But he figured that there weren't official police circles in Willowsdown but simply townsfolk looking out for the good of each other with him, Chief Goodman, as the badged facilitator. When 13 years ago Mrs. Montgomery's son, Leland, died, the chief at that time had pointed a finger at a young fellow accusing him of murder or at least manslaughter. It was Mrs. Montgomery, Leland's own mother, who drew attention to the facts and circumstances that clearly proved it was

a case of accidental death. He, himself, as sergeant had
been so thoroughly impressed by Mrs. Montgomery's
reasoning abilities and notice of details that he told
himself if ever there was a time he could help her he
would. Last December with the kerfuffle over the stolen
brooch and the funeral director's suspicious death he
had been more than willing to collaborate with Mrs.
Montgomery. His decision had proven to be a wise one.
It seemed to him to be short-sighted not to put her skills
to use just because she wasn't official. He, on the other
hand, *was* considered official and in that capacity it was
his responsibility to tell Frances and Elspeth Roberts
that the death of Mr. Roberts was now considered a
case of murder and therefore they must not leave town.
Without tasting it, he took another swallow of coffee,
set his mug on the counter and clapped the police cap
on his head. He liked it so much better when the week
started out and his most trying case was the theft of Bill
Wainfleet's bike which had turned up on its own
anyway.

While waiting in line at George Flesherton's butcher
shop, Dorothea had fallen into a reverie and was letting
the conversation ebb and flow unheedingly around her.
There was a longer line than usual because George's
assistant, Alex Kaminen, had left on Thursday
afternoon to take the train to Port Arthur.

Alex was George's cousin on his mother's side.
George's mother's sister had married a lumber mill
fellow from Port Arthur and moved with him to the far
north. George and Alex had met only once years ago
when George had stayed with his aunt and her family
while he, along with Alex, planted trees as a summer
job. A backbreaking job which made joining the family
butcher business much more palatable. In those summer
months, and with the camaraderie born of shared

misery, a stalwart friendship had developed between George and Alex. So, when George's mother shared her sister's letter outlining a devastating financial hardship caused by a swindle costing the family the loss of their lumber mill, George immediately offered a job to his cousin, Alex. It had turned out to be an inspired decision. Alex, along with many of the other Finnish residents, had always enjoyed Finnish pancakes at The Hoito, Port Arthur's signature community restaurant. George had also eaten his share of Hoito pancakes but it had never occurred to him to spread the yumminess when back in Willowsdown. When Alex joined George in the butcher shop, he came up with a flavour mix for sausage that paired deliciously with Finnish pancakes. The pancake recipe (from Alex's Finnish grandmother) was included with an order for the sausage. It had been a hit. The Imperial included the pancakes and sausages on its menu and many of the exclusively English or Scottish homes of Willowsdown added some international flavour to their palates. Alex, himself was a well-liked fellow. He was very tall and robustly built. The townspeople fondly referred to him as their gentle giant as he was soft spoken and easy going. He wasn't able to get home to Port Arthur very often but George insisted he go as often as possible. Hence his absence as of Thursday.

Dorothea's reverie was in fact focused on gentle giant Alex wondering how his mother was faring. The shock of the swindle and loss of the mill had caused a massive heart attack in Alex's father which subsequently took his life. Alex lived very frugally in order to send as much money as possible to his mother. Dorothea hoped Mrs. Kaminen would agree to move to Willowsdown. With her husband gone and her son and sister here, it seemed to Dorothea to be sensible to return south. The sisters might as well share their widowhoods.

"Mrs. Montgomery, what can I do for you today?"

Somehow Dorothea's turn had come up. She felt a little embarrassed that she had managed to move through the line surrounded by others and not said a word to anyone.

"Hello, George. Charles is wondering about wild turkeys. Have any come in?"

"Absolutely. How many would he like?"

"Oh, I should think one would be sufficient."

"Well he's in luck as a few came in fresh today. They're just hanging in the cooler. I can send one around later this afternoon if you'd like."

"That will be fine."

"Not entirely sure what time that'll be as the young fellow filling in for Alex is green at this though he sure seems to have caught on quick. I told Alex yesterday it didn't seem to me that he needed to shadow his replacement on The Imperial order but you know Alex; he wants to be sure of a good job. He could have taken an earlier train had he not insisted. Anyhow, so far today no orders have gone astray so I'm sure yours will show up just fine. Are you going to want the bird plucked?"

"Yes, Mrs. White would be glad for that. This is Dianna's day working at The Imperial otherwise she could help. So, go ahead with the plucking but leave the scalding for Mrs. White."

"Done!"

"While I'm here I'll take some liver. I do so hate it and Mrs. White is not at all happy at how it smells up the kitchen but Charles loves it so he's indulged occasionally. Let this be the occasion. I've got my string bag here in my purse somewhere."

Handing over the squishy parcel, George said, "Don't forget the onions!"

"No worries there. Mrs. White always has plenty on hand." A line had formed again behind her. Turning to leave, she said, "It's hard to believe you used to do this by yourself."

"It sure is. Alex has been a real boon. Give my greetings to Mr. Montgomery. I'm with him on the liver."

When Chief Goodman arrived at The Imperial to report to Mrs. and Miss Roberts that Mr. Roberts' death was considered suspicious and that they were to stay in town, he was told by the hotel clerk that neither woman was in the hotel at the moment.

"Gadding about," he muttered gruffly to himself. It used to be that when you wanted to talk with a woman she'd be at home and you didn't have to wander to and fro over the whole earth. He recognized he was being unreasonable but frankly he wasn't happy about having a murder on his hands.

"Well, then, I'm heading on up to the suite. Got some more scouring to do. Thanks," he said as the room key was handed to him.

In the suite, he pocketed the key and stood in the entranceway surveying the room. The afternoon light was streaming through the three floor-to-ceiling windows. The white of the carpet and couches glowed under its ministrations. The mantelpiece was flowingly carved but had been painted white and it too glowed. It was a bright room. Seemed hard to believe something as dark as murder had taken place here. He removed his shoes and tiptoed across the carpet. The slight smudges on the wall to the left of the mantelpiece were just barely visible as were the discoloured spots on the carpet. So why were there bloodstains here and yet Mr.

Roberts clearly broke his neck falling down the stairs? He turned toward the staircase. He crouched over slightly to better examine the carpet between the mantel and the staircase and walked over slowly, weaving back and forth in case someone heading to the staircase didn't walk in a straight line. No blood stains. Which he already knew as there had been none the day Mr. Roberts was found. Upstairs then. Again, he examined carefully as he mounted the stairs in case something had been previously missed. Nothing. Further examination of the two bedrooms yielded nothing.

"A whole lot of nothing," muttered Chief Goodman as he stepped into the study. After fingerprinting and photographing, the chief and Nelson Jr. had removed all the papers from the desk to examine them more closely at the station. The chief reminded himself that still needed to be done. There wouldn't be blood here because he and Mrs. Montgomery had peered closely. But since it seemed to him that the study was Mr. Roberts' domain, this would be the most likely place to find hidden alcohol. He knew there wasn't any in the desk because that had already been cleared. A trap door in the mantelpiece? Unlikely. He sheepishly moved the loveseat and chairs in the sitting area to be sure nothing was hidden under them. It seemed foolish but one never knows. And then there was the bookshelf. He began removing books. It was on a shelf where the books were not pushed to the back that he discovered behind them a glass and a bottle of whiskey. He noticed another shelf where the books were perched on the edge and there too he found a small bottle of brandy and some rye.

"Whew," he blew through his teeth. "So, he *had* been drinking. Wonder where he was getting the stuff."

He plucked out his handkerchief for handling the glass and three bottles and carefully placed them on the desk. He would have Nelson Jr. collect them and bring them to the station for fingerprinting. If there should happen to be prints besides Mr. Roberts' it just might point to … what? Well something, anyway.

After handing over the unwanted meat to Mrs. White who rolled her eyes and wrinkled her nose, Dorothea wandered into the morning room. Her eye caught the manila envelope that Dianna had brought to her after finding it at the hotel.

"Vermont!"

She tugged it out and headed to the phone in the front hall.

"Hello, Elva. Please put me through to the police station."

"Goodman here."

"Oh good. I was hoping you were there. I have something to show you. May I bring it over?"

"Does it have to do with Roberts' death?"

"Maybe."

"I'll be here."

"Well, I'll be," said Chief Goodman rubbing his bald head after Dorothea showed him the foolscap sheet of paper.

"Do you think it could have anything to do with whiskey running?"

"I'll show you what I found in Mr. Roberts' bookshelf."

He removed the bottles from a cupboard and lined them up on the desk.

"I wouldn't have thought of Vermont as a hotbed of illegal alcohol," said Dorothea, nodding to the sheet of paper.

"Maybe its unlikeliness is its cover."

"But the Roberts are from Minnesota."

Chief Goodman shrugged.

"So are we actually looking for a stranger who slipped in and killed Mr. Roberts?" asked Dorothea.

"Don't know. But this whiskey running stuff can be dangerous—people are definitely killed. There's a nasty gang in Hamilton headed up by one Rocco Perri. The police in Waterloo have confirmed that that bunch and even Al Capone's crew run in and out of there."

Dorothea stared at him.

"We get reports occasionally so we're in the loop," he explained.

"You haven't actually had to deal with any of this, have you?"

"No. And I hope we aren't starting now."

"I just had a horrid thought. Why was the Wainfleet house rummaged? Surely they aren't involved?"

The chief said slowly, "I suppose a stationmaster would be a good person to have on an illegal payroll."

Both sets of eyes turned back to the sheet outlining, among other things, train depots.

"No. I won't believe it," stated Dorothea.

"Someone was in their house. That's still a fact. I'm going to have to do my own search," he said grimly.

"If," began Dorothea miserably, "they are involved, wouldn't they be tipped off, or whatever the saying is, and move anything that needed moving?"

"Likely but I still need to try."

They sat in unhappy silence.

Dorothea brightened.

"But surely they wouldn't have been so eager to move Joe into their house that evening if they had something to hide. They would have known you would be called in."

Chief Goodman perked up.

"You might have something there. I'll start with finding out where they each were when Mr. Roberts was killed. If I can eliminate them from that part of the situation that'll be a good day's work. The rest I'll look into later."

Chapter Six

That evening after Charles ate liver and onions and
Dorothea did not, the two of them were sitting in front
of a fire in the library balancing trays on their laps
laden with coffee and rhubarb pie. Their dog, Lily, had
snuggled in beside Dorothea. The way she and the chief
had ended their meeting had heartened her and so she
was able to turn her mind for the moment to more
pleasant things.

"What do you think then? The electric refrigerator
will be here on Monday. That will mean it will be easier
to make the ice cream since Dilman won't have to chip
ice off the ice block. Mrs. White can simply set aside a
large amount of ice cubes to use in the ice-cream
maker. The salesman showed me the ice cube trays that
come with the freezer part of the refrigerator. I don't
know how long it takes for them to freeze but if we start
a few days ahead, it should be enough time," said
Dorothea.

"Ice cream is a great idea. The Little 'Uns will love
it. Let's get Mrs. White to make some chocolate sauce
and we'll throw on some peanuts and it'll feel like
we're at a soda fountain," agreed Charles.

"The Little 'Uns will love it! I'm thinking that
Grandpa will not be far behind," teased Dorothea.

"Great invention—ice-cream."

A few months back, Dorothea and Charles had
purchased 40 acres of land just outside of town—two
acres cleared and 38 acres bush. A creek ran through
the property and there was a small house at the front of
the cleared area. Charles envisioned a Boy Scout/Girl

Guide camp being set up there. In the meantime, they had hired a retired couple to keep up the property. The house needed some loving care but the reason this particular couple had been hired as caretakers was because they were entirely capable of making the necessary renovations. The wife of the couple was green thumbed and would put in a market garden. With an eye to the future of the property, Charles had set the man the task of digging a double outhouse hole and building the outhouse itself on the cleared part of the land close to the bush, the idea being that whenever the camp took shape, the necessary facilities would be up and running so to speak. In the meantime, with that amount of land to care for, the couple would appreciate the facility whenever they were in "the back forty". The ice-cream was needed for the ribbon cutting ceremony that Dorothea and Charles were planning for the outhouse. "Aunt Jane's" as they dubbed it.

"I'll get some bunting for draping Aunt Jane's and we'll use the pots and pans and spoons to create a suitable clamour," continued Dorothea.

"Leland and Simon and I will make some paper hats. Do you think Magdala and Lucy will want grass skirts?"

"I know they will. They've already been talking about it."

Dorothea and Charles had shared their ribbon cutting ceremony idea with their grandchildren, the Little 'Uns, who were thrilled with the idea.

"I think you should lead the parade with some kind of conductor's baton," said Dorothea. "Would Dilman be able to whittle something out of a branch of some sort?"

"I've no doubt he could," mumbled Charles through a mouthful of pie.

A head poked around the library doorway.

"Mr. North! Come and sit. Is everything all right with Joe?" Dorothea asked in sudden alarm.

"All right in the sense that he's no worse," replied Mr. North, removing his hat. "He did come to briefly this afternoon which is a good sign. But Elva is close on my heels and will tell you more. I just came with a recipe idea for the Girl Guide cookies."

"Have some pie, man," urged Charles nodding to the remaining pieces.

"I put the nose bag on at home. I'm full up." Mr. North smiled, rubbing his stomach. "You'll want a basic recipe since you'll be baking up a lot."

Dorothea nodded.

"Here's a sugar cookie recipe with a twist—allspice in the batter and sprinkled with vanilla sugar. Easy to roll out, cut out and pop in the oven. I always have a bowl of sugar with a vanilla bean stirred in so I have vanilla sugar on hand. You won't need too much as you're just sprinkling it. What do you think?" he asked, handing over the scrap of paper torn from brown wrapping paper on which he had scribbled the recipe.

Dorothea scanned the list of ingredients. "Well, I think that will be wonderful!" she replied enthusiastically. "Each Guide can bake four or five dozen at home and bring them out to the Victoria Day festivities. That should raise a reasonable amount towards uniforms and camping equipment."

"Let me know how many girls will be baking and I'll get an employee to package up small bags of the vanilla sugar they'll need. They can come by and get their parcels when needed. It'll be my contribution to the effort."

"Thank you, Mr. North. I'm getting excited about this! In fact, maybe I'll bake a practice batch for next weekend when Leland, Magdala, Simon and Lucy are here for the ribbon cutting at Aunt Jane's."

Mr. North looked at her quizzically.

Charles grinned. "The outhouse at the new property. We're having a parade with our grandchildren to celebrate its grand opening."

"Ah. Well," said Mr. North, returning his brimmed hat to his head, "time and tide wait for no man. I should think Elva will be along any minute."

"We'll look forward to seeing her," said Dorothea.

They had returned to their seats after shaking hands with their guest and Dorothea just finished saying, "I wonder what our Elva girl has on her mind," when said young woman appeared in the doorway with a cherry red cloche hat on her blonde, bobbed head.

Elva was the youngest in a family of five children with four brothers ahead of her. The three oldest brothers were married and living in and around Willowsdown. Joe was the brother next to her. They had always been close. There was nothing that Joe and her other brothers did that Elva didn't do also. She had determinedly toddled after them as soon as she could walk and took her share of scrapes and bruises like the trooper she was. When after her oldest brother went to law school and, on his weekends home practiced his legal "cases" on the family, she astonished everyone with her incisive questioning. Dorothea and Charles had known Elva all her life but from a distance. It wasn't until their great nephew, George Seyler, surprised them all by announcing that he wasn't returning home to England with his sister and his grandmother after their extended visit at Christmas—and the reason he wasn't going was Elva.

George, Dorothea and Charles discovered, was a kind and generous fellow though rather narrow in his outlook. He had been born with the proverbial silver spoon in his mouth, attending all the "right" schools and hobnobbing with England's jet set. He had accompanied his grandmother to Canada really more for a lark than anything but when he encountered Elva's energetic thinking and broader outlook it felt like a sunlit window being flung open in a dark room. And Elva had discerned that George possessed a deeper character than he himself had yet plumbed. Since March when their engagement was announced Elva had often visited as Dorothea and Charles were George's only family. Now Elva was "our Elva girl".

Charles stood as Elva entered and indicated his chair. "Sit here, Elva. Lily and I are due for a walk."

The bundle of white fluffiness had jumped to the floor with a wagging tail when Elva walked in and now sped up the wagging at the mention of a walk.

"Come on, girl. Let's you and I count stars. See you in a bit, ladies."

"How are you, my dear?" asked Dorothea warmly after Charles and Lily left and Elva had settled in. "Would you like anything?"

"Oh, no, nothing at all, thank you. I'm all right. Tired though. It was busy at the phone exchange office today. Well, it always is on a Friday but the death of Mr. Roberts certainly lit up the board. I think too that gossip is wearing."

"True."

"And then Joe, of course. I can't stand to see him just lying there; it's so unnatural. He's always full of curiosity and bursting with ideas. Now he's so pale and quiet. He did come to for a bit this afternoon though. George was with him."

"Oh?"

"Yes. During the office tea break he popped over to sit with Joe. He's been doing that as much as he can. He thinks that talking to Joe about everyday things will help Joe to come back to us. He was chatting that way this afternoon when Joe opened his eyes. George said it was like he was focusing his eyes and then he said, 'Hey George.' Then he was silent although he was looking at George and then he blurted out, 'Stop!' and that was all. He shut his eyes and was quiet again."

"You know, as small as that is, it's significant. He hasn't known George very long and yet he recognized him. I would think that's a good sign."

Elva sat up a bit straighter. "I was hoping you would say that. That's what I've been thinking."

"What did Dr. Payne say?"

"He hasn't had a chance to come by yet today. Mother is expecting him yet this evening though."

"Did George tell you about Joe?"

Elva blushed. "He did. He stopped by the exchange office on his way back to work. But Mother also told me because she was there at the time."

Dorothea sat silently with her hands folded in her lap. She wasn't going to say anything more about George or the broken off engagement. The way that Elva was fiddling with the tassel at the end of her dress sash indicated to her that by waiting, Elva herself would get to it.

"Mrs. Montgomery …"

Dorothea wanted to say, "You mean Aunt Dorothea," but she didn't. As much as she hoped she would be Elva's Aunt Dorothea, the situation as it stood was that at this moment she wasn't.

"I hear you were asking about Elspeth today at the library."

Dorothea hadn't expected this. She had been hoping to hear about a reconciliation with George slated for the near future. It could only have been Miss Weber who had reported on her—she knew Miss Kabfleisch wouldn't.

"Ah, well, yes, I was."

"May I ask why?" Before Dorothea could answer, Elva continued, "The reason Dr. Payne couldn't get to Joe sooner is because he was doing an autopsy on Mr. Roberts. An autopsy means that the cause of death is questioned. Since Chief Goodman is involved, there must be a question of criminal involvement. Is that true?"

Dorothea opened her mouth and shut it again. Her first impulse was to ask, 'and just how did you hear that an autopsy was being performed?' But, really, in a small town what would be the point in asking the question? Who could fathom how it was that confidential activities ended up in the open? As far as she knew, there was no way Mrs. Johnson could have heard. But then, there were so many unexplained things in this world. Instead she said, "Yes, that is true."

"And that's why you were asking questions about Elspeth?"

"I'm afraid so."

"I wish you wouldn't."

"Why not?"

"It will only make things worse!" Elva stood up suddenly.

"What things?"

"Oh! I don't know why it is that people have to fall in love!" she blurted and hurried out of the room.

Dorothea got up to follow her but decided against it.

"'Ours is not to reason why,'" murmured Dorothea to herself and the fire.

Chief Goodman just wanted to sit at home this evening. He just wanted a cup of his wife's cocoa and a crossword puzzle. Instead he was standing at the front door of people he liked and respected intending to ask them questions that smacked of his being suspicious of their role in the death of a stranger. This was not the way he wanted to finish out a day. He sighed and knocked reluctantly snatching his cap off his head.

"Good evening, Chief," said Anna Wainfleet warmly when she opened the door. "You've just caught me. I was heading over to see how Joe is doing."

"I'll try not to keep you long but I do need to speak a moment with you and Bill."

"Well, come in. Would you like something to drink— —tea or coffee?"

"Neither, thanks."

"Your boots are fine there. Bill isn't in right now. It's his bowling night."

"Right. I had forgotten that. I have some questions to ask you both about Thursday. The day Mr. Roberts, the American visitor died. Just routine," he said squirming a bit on his seat.

"About Mr. Roberts? Well, I didn't even know him to see him."

"If I could just know what you were doing between 4:30 and 5:45 that afternoon it will help me to corroborate other, ah, other theories." He was rather proud of himself for the way he phrased his inquiry— that didn't sound too much like he was suspicious of something.

"Oh. Well, I was at the church hall. The WI ladies were finishing up a batch of rhubarb jam. As a matter of fact we were a bit behind as there had been a wee accident and clean up took much longer so it was just before 6:00 before we all locked up and left."

"There were others with you?"

She looked at him a trifle disgustedly. It would seem she was getting the gist of his inquiries. "Of course there were. Shall I name them?"

"That won't be necessary."

"I suppose you want to ask Bill the same question?"

"Yes."

"That's easy. He was at the station. On Thursdays there's the 4:20 coming into town and the 5:35 leaving town. He always stays between the trains."

"Right. Bill's movements are pretty easy to detect," he said at an attempt at humour.

"He takes great pride in his job," said Anna.

"We're lucky to have him. Thank you, Anna. That helps to patch up some holes in, ah, some proposed theories."

"I hope so. Unpleasant business for everyone."

"Yep. I won't need to talk to Bill after all. If Joe is conscious, tell him I say hello. I hope to get over soon."

"I will. He'll understand that this'll be taking up your time."

"Right then. Thanks again for your time," he said quickly slipping on his boots. He halfheartedly, and hopefully discreetly, looked around the hallway for signs of a secret compartment and then bid her good night.

Chapter Seven

The Saturday of the Victoria Day weekend always began the market season in Willowsdown. Farmers brought in meat and fruit and vegetables and handmade cheese. The earliest offering was rhubarb but since rhubarb poked up profusely in so many yards in town there wasn't too much to be seen at the market itself. It was the asparagus that Dorothea's mouth watered for. Last spring Mrs. White had served an asparagus omelet with wild leeks and a soft cheese she had made. Surfacing from a deep sleep this Saturday morning—a week from the hope of asparagus—Dorothea had been dreaming the taste of that deliciousness and awoke with disappointment considering her awareness of the calendar.

"As Winnie the Pooh says, 'botheration'!" she muttered. "That would've been just the thing this morning."

The Victoria Day planning meeting that had been scheduled for Thursday evening, the night Mr. Roberts had been found, had been rescheduled for later that morning. Even suspicious death could not keep the celebrations from happening. There were final details that needed, well, finalizing, particularly in regards to parade arrangements. Out of respect for Frances and Elspeth Roberts—assuming innocence until proven guilty—Chief Goodman requested that the meeting be held on the second floor of the market building rather than at The Imperial.

Dorothea had tossed and turned during the night and had allowed herself a sleep in. Charles had already left to do something—she couldn't remember what and he would meet her at the meeting. *Wild turkey*, she thought randomly, *I suppose that's what Mrs. White will prepare for supper.* From wild turkey, her mind meandered to hunters which then took her to open spaces which then took her to their property outside of town which then took her to the Aunt Jane's christening which then took her to grass skirts. *I'll need to gather up some straw to use for the grass skirts*, she mused. *Brown's farm, I think. I'll ask Muriel about it today at the meeting.* She continued to lie in bed musing over nothing in particular but not feeling energized enough to get up. It wasn't long though, until the wafting of coffee and warm cinnamon from the few leftover cinnamon buns drew her from her bed.

The group of townspeople that sat around the table in the market building included Ambrose North, Elva North, Muriel Brown from whom Dorothea needed grass skirt making straw, George Flesherton, Mrs. Johnson, Dr. Caleb Withrow, the town's vet, Isaac Kingswood, the town's blacksmith, Arthur Poole, the town's funeral director Chief Goodman, Dorothea and Charles, and George Seyler, their grandnephew. George had maneuvered to get a chair close to Elva but somehow, she had outmaneuvered him and he was at the extreme end of the table from her. Ambrose North's offering of bread and jam had been enjoyed down to the last crumb and spoonful and happily between mouthfuls, decisions had, in fact, been agreed upon.

Beyond the festive mood that always accompanied the Victoria Day preparations, there were, according to Dorothea's reckoning, a few undercurrents. To her, of course, the most evident of undercurrents were between

Elva and George. George had been doggedly trying to catch Elva's eye while Elva just as doggedly refused to look his way. That is, she refused to look his way except when she knew he was, in courtesy and attentiveness, looking at someone else. Another was the faint heaviness exuding from Ambrose North in concern for his still unconscious grandson, Joe. Unusual from the enthusiastic man but there it was nonetheless. And then a whiff of—what was it?—triumph perhaps? That though a man had been struck dead amongst them it had certainly no connection with any of the folk of Willowsdown. Since it could only have been the American wife or daughter no one need feel the unease of suspicion towards one another and therefore no reason not to enjoy the coming festivities. They were just finalizing the order of the parade with the decision to round it off with war veterans when Chief Goodman's youngest son came panting up the steps and across the hardwood floor.

"Dad! Joe North is awake and asking for you. His mom sent me to get you."

"For me?"

"Yeah. He's got something to tell you."

"Right. Excuse me everyone." The Chief scraped back his chair, tousled his son's hair and, snatching his hat and jacket from the coat rack by the door, left the group exclaiming and wondering to each other. Why should the chief be the first person Joe wanted to talk to? Could it be Joe saw who stole Bill Wainfleet's bike? Or better yet who broke into the Wainfleet home?

"Ladies and gentlemen! Ladies and gentlemen!" Charles voiced over the questioning din. "This is good news about Joe. Let's leave our speculations for the chief's attention. We'll look forward to further hopeful reports on Joe's health and in the meantime are we agreed then that the veterans will round out the parade? Raise your hand for aye."

Every hand around the table was raised.

"The ayes have it. Thanks everyone. If there's nothing else, I believe we're done here."

The group quickly gathered up personal belongings with the pleasant excitement of insider knowledge. Mrs. Johnson who usually tarried and chatted, excused herself with a wave of her hand. "Duty calls. I mustn't neglect the myriad of tasks that accompany enterprise." Muriel Brown, buttoned her coat rapidly while Dorothea explained her need for straw to make grass skirts with her granddaughters. "Certainly, Mrs. Montgomery, that'll be fine. Come out whenever you need it. It's always there." (It wasn't until later that evening when Muriel and her husband had a chance to sit down after chores and she was recounting the events of the day, that she realized she had no idea what it was that Mrs. Montgomery wanted that straw for.) In varying degrees of urgency, it was the same for everyone who left the meeting.

"Excuse me, Mr. North," said George. "I imagine you and Miss North would like to see Joe. I have my car. May I offer you a ride?"

Mr. North clapped George on the shoulder. "You're a gentleman and a scholar and there's mighty few of us left. I'll accept your offer, George. Will you, Elva?"

Elva looked between the two men and nodded her acceptance.

George helped her on with her coat.

"Thank you, George," she said quietly.

George considered the thanks to cover the car and the coat.

"Well!" said Dorothea as she and Charles strolled home. "I wonder what Joe wanted to tell Chief Goodman?"

"You'll be the first to know."

"Possibly. Everyone will soon have their ear to the ground. I do wonder though…"

"Yes?"

Dorothea stopped and tilted her head. "That night when I was walking, I remember hearing a shout in the distance. At the time I thought it was someone calling for a dog named 'Spot' or even I had supposed someone yelling 'stop'. I wonder … maybe it was Joe shouting 'stop'. Maybe he did see someone and that someone hit him over the head."

"Well … maybe. That's a bit farfetched. A bit too much imagination I'd say."

"Hmph." Dorothea began walking again. "Well something out of the ordinary happened because there was Joe unconscious on the railway line."

"True. There's no use speculating, Dorothea; it will just muddle your thinking."

"I'm not speculating. I'm imagining scenarios which doesn't cause muddle. It allows for creative possibilities."

"Hmph," replied Charles.

"Elspeth," began Frances Roberts. "What did you see when you were at the library the day your father—died?" Frances was pacing restlessly about the living area of their new suite and Elspeth was reading, apparently.

"What do you mean?"

"You were sitting in the window."

"How do you know?"

"Does that matter?"

"I just saw people walking about downtown."

"Anyone in particular?"

"We don't really know anyone in town but I didn't see you."

Frances paused in her pacing and scrutinized her daughter.

"When I began my walk, I left by the back private entrance but then I changed my mind about where I wanted to go and I circled back and passed the library. You weren't in the window seat then."

"I was looking at books. It's what one does in a library."

"And what about Thomas? Have you heard from him?"

The book that Elspeth had lowered to her lap slid to the floor. She picked it up slowly.

"You mean a letter?"

"I mean in any way. I thought perhaps you had and that's why you and your father argued earlier that afternoon."

"I wasn't the only one who argued with him that day." Elspeth fingered her pearl bangles.

"Why did you take the handkerchief? I saw the initials."

"That has nothing to do with this!"

Elspeth jumped up, the book thudding on the carpet. "I can't stay here! It's too horrible! I'm going to ask Chief Goodman if I can stay with Elva North."

"Elspeth ..." Frances reached out a hand.

"No! This is a nightmare."

Elspeth trod on the book in her dash to the door. She flung it open and it banged against the wall.

Frances walked slowly to the door and gazed down the hallway. Elspeth was already at the steps and didn't look back. *It will be easier this way*, she thought, as she firmly shut the door.

As it turned out, Muriel Brown needed to stop at the Emporium so she called to Mrs. Johnson as that energetic lady made her swift way onto the street.

"Mrs. Johnson! I'm heading your way."

"What do you think? Did Joe see someone?"

Mrs. Johnson never let subtlety get in the way of knowledge.

"Well, it's so hard to say but I suppose why else would he want to talk to the police?"

"Precisely. Let me consider. Joe was stumbled upon in his maimed condition..."

"I don't think he could be called maimed," broke in Mrs. Brown.

"Disadvantaged then," continued Mrs. Johnson, "on Wednesday evening."

"I clearly remember it wasn't a pleasant evening because Everett and I were very keen to be indoors when the chores were done."

"Exactly. So, there would have been few people out and about."

"We know Mrs. Montgomery was out because she found Joe."

"As were Mr. and Mrs. Wainfleet. It would be conducive to helpfulness on behalf of the chief if I questioned them as to whom they saw."

Mrs. Brown worked out what Mrs. Johnson meant and replied, "He'll come to that himself. No need to muddy the waters. More to the point is what meetings were gathered that night. If we know what meetings there were, we'll know who was out and about."

"Precisely."

The two women continued in their stride and considered.

"I don't think there were any," said Mrs. Brown after some thought.

"I think you're right. How annoying. But wait! Why didn't I think of this before!" Mrs. Johnson stopped and seized the arm of her companion. "Just guess who I saw that evening!"

"Um..."

"Mr. Roberts!"

"Mr. Roberts?"

"Yes! Mr. Roberts was talking with Alex Kaminen. This is what happened. I had gone home after closing up. But then recalled I had meant to take home a jar of pickles so I returned, commandeered the pickles and spied that the bundle of forsythia in the window had toppled so I straightened it and as I did so I spotted the two men conferencing on the sidewalk!" She finished almost exultantly.

"And?"

"And, one of them could have just stolen Mr. Wainfleet's bike and clobbered Joe or were on their way to do so."

"But ..."

"OR they were in collusion."

"Why on earth would either of them want a bike or to injure Joe? Mr. Roberts was just passing through and Alex is still fairly new to the town."

"Precisely."

"Precisely? Whatever do you mean?"

"We don't know that much about Alex."

"He's George Flesherton's cousin, for heaven's sake."

"Oh. Yes. You're right." Mrs. Johnson looked crestfallen. "Perhaps I got a bit carried away."

"You certainly did! Stick to what you know." They had reached the Grocery Emporium. "You know this," said Mrs. Brown, waving to the store's sign. "Now tell me, Everett is already about sick of rhubarb desserts, do you have any suggestions?"

"Ah, now. I deem I have just the thing! Do you still have dried apples?"

"Yes."

"I scrutinized a recipe just the other day. Fry your apples in butter, sprinkle with sugar and cinnamon, pile them on top of a molasses cake and pinnacle it with whipped cream!"

"Thank you, that'll definitely do the trick. Lead me to the molasses."

Chapter Eight

Elspeth buttoned her cardigan jacket and balled her hands in the pockets. *What an idiot to race out without a coat,* she thought, but, she straightened her spine as the comforting thought came to her, Elva will have what I need. Passing North's Bakery, in her flight to the police station, she glanced in the window. Seeing a young woman behind the counter she turned in.

"Good afternoon. May I help you?" asked Nellie Goodman, Chief Goodman's 16-year-old daughter.

"I, well, I'm not sure."

"We close in half an hour so there isn't much left," explained Nellie apologetically.

"Oh, that's all right. I was just feeling a little chilly."

Nellie looked over the stylishly dressed young woman, only a few years older than herself. She did seem cold. Nellie wondered why she was out without a coat and hat and gloves. It was May, yes, but still nippy. She also wondered where she was going because she knew this was Elspeth Roberts, daughter of the murdered American.

The girls eyed each other over the counter until Elspeth looked past Nellie into the kitchen.

"Would you like an Empire cookie? I made the batter myself."

Nellie pulled out a tray of the jam-filled, iced sandwich cookies with their cheery cherry settled in the centre.

Elspeth's gaze was drawn back and focused on the sweet offering.

"They do look good."

"I can fix you a cup of tea to go with it if you'd like."

Elspeth seemed to be listening for something but then smiled saying, "I would like that."

"Just sit yourself down."

North's Bakery didn't cater to sit down customers but there was one table at the end of the counter for those customers who just needed to take a load off their feet.

As she sat, Elspeth suddenly wanted to cry. What was she doing? A cookie and a cup of tea couldn't fix the terrible dilemma she was in. And how could she draw Elva into it? It wasn't as though she and Elva were long time bosom friends. They had met by chance two weeks ago at the library when they both reached for the same book. From there they had chatted pretty much every day as they found their hearts and minds had much in common. If she took refuge with Elva, she would have to tell her *some*thing. But to whom else could she turn? Certainly not to the one other person she knew in town.

Nellie had placed two cookies on a plate and set it in front of Elspeth.

"If you don't eat them both now, you'll have a readymade treat for later. No, no," Nellie said holding up her hands as Elspeth fumbled in her pocket for change both girls knew probably wasn't there, "consider it an end-of-the-day special. I'm sure that's what Mr. North would want."

"Thank you."

"I'll just get the tea going."

Elspeth examined the unfamiliar cookie and carefully took a bite.

From the kitchen, Nellie called out the back door, "Nat! When you're done with the garbage, come in and help me clean the mixer." She measured out the tea as the kettle came to a boil. She figured that once Miss Roberts was enjoying her tea, Nat could take care of any customers and she would nip out the back door to the police station and just let her dad know that one of his suspects had left the hotel. She wasn't sure that it mattered. It was more likely that leaving town was the problem. But it was rather exciting to think she might be helping him with a case. She and Nelson Jr. had seen a movie once, one out of the two movies they'd ever seen, where a detective was helped in solving a case when someone nonchalantly kept the suspect chatting about everyday things giving the detective time to come and make an arrest. She couldn't help thinking that there was something suspicious about Miss Roberts being out without a coat and hat and so on. Especially without a hat. A thrilling quiver raced down her spine as she reached for a cup and saucer. She placed them and the teapot on a tray and headed into the storefront.

"Well! Where is she?" she said aloud. There was one cookie left on the plate but no Elspeth.

"Nat!" She turned on her heel. Setting the tray on the kneading table, she poked her head out the back door. "Nat, I've got to get to the police station! You take care of the store."

"Oh. Okay. Is there something wrong?"

"I can't say. Police business."

Nat stifled a smile. "Right. Well, you'd best be off." He good naturedly gave her a salute.

"I won't be long." And with that, she rattled down the back steps still swinging on her coat, but not her hat, and sprinted to the police station.

She dashed in the back door at the station, panting with important news only to hear Elspeth's voice at the front of the station asking Nelson Jr. if Chief Goodman was available.

Chief Goodman, was not available as he was sitting beside Joe North's bed in a room with the blinds drawn to keep the light from aggravating Joe's aching head. He had been carefully documenting what Joe slowly shared.

"Let me make sure I have this right, Joe," said the chief rifling through his notes. "You were heading home about 7:30 p.m. As you neared the tracks across from the Wainfleet house you saw a man hop on Bill Wainfleet's bike and steer it onto the street."

"Yes."

"And you say this man was wearing a military uniform."

"Yes."

"At that time of the evening the light is dim so it can be tricky. Are you sure?"

"Without a doubt."

"A military uniform—hmmm."

"I yelled for him to stop. I started after him and," Joe flagged a bit.

"That's when you tripped and hit your head. Go easy, son. You've tired yourself with giving me your statement. For whatever reason, the bike was left at a neighbour's place. So officially it isn't stolen. Finding the military man is the thing now. Just rest. Junior and I'll take care of it."

"Only one possibility…" Joe offered weakly.

"Yep," agreed the chief, reaching for his cap. "Rest up and get strong. We all miss you."

On his way to The Imperial, Chief Goodman passed the blacksmith shop. Isaac Kingswood and his wife, Olive, were sitting outside, both of them with grimy faces. Isaac and Olive were very recently married and it still made him chuckle to see them together as Olive was a young woman from a lot of money and during the week kept her hands very clean at her job as one of the operators at the town's phone and telegraph exchange office along with Elva. But occasionally she could be seen all grubbed up with her husband at the blacksmith shop. This was one of those times.

"You have a different helper today, Isaac," said Chief Goodman, grinning.

Olive laughed. "I think I'm actually getting good at this. Philip better watch his back."

"This is one of Philip's days to work with Bill at the station," said Isaac.

"How does that seem to be going? asked the chief.

"Pretty good, I think. Kind of wondering if he might be preferring it to this," said Isaac. "When Bill wanted Philip to cover him for a bit on Thursday, Philip was off like a shot. Good thing I wasn't in need of a second pair of hands."

Chief Goodman stiffened.

"On Thursday this was? What time was that?"

Isaac took a swig of Canada Dry and considered. "Well ... I'm thinking it was about 5:00 or so. He was only gone half an hour or so."

"I see. Alright, thanks," he said morosely and left them abruptly.

"What was that all about?" asked Olive.

Isaac shrugged.

"Don't know."

"Oh well," said Olive, clinking her Canada Dry bottle against Isaac's.

"Slainte," said the newlyweds together taking a swallow of the champagne of ginger ales and looking into each other's eyes.

Chief Goodman continued down the street with a heavy heart and at The Imperial he ran his finger down the pages of the hotel's sign-in register. He was looking for the name of the fellow who had been living in Room 201. The hotel's manager knew the military man had been in that room; he just couldn't remember his name. Ah. There it was. Thomas Nathaniels. Now he had to contact the Canadian Armed Forces and track down this Thomas Nathaniels. *Oh joy*, he thought. That'll be about as much fun as having a tooth pulled except it'll take 36,000 times longer. On the other hand, now that the war had been over for almost 10 years he wasn't sure what the military did with their time. That was a cheering thought. They might be glad to have something to do. And while they did that he would look into the Bill Wainfleet question. He was going to assume that Anna truly did not know that Bill had left his post on Thursday and just concentrate on Bill. After, that is, he faced Mrs. Roberts.

He was going to offer the Roberts women every courtesy accorded to a grieving family even though they were under suspicion of murder. Except for the possibility of a whiskey running stranger who so far had entirely eluded being seen by anyone anywhere near the hotel or anywhere in the town for that matter. He really wasn't too sure about the existence of such a person. But had Bill provided cover for such a person? He shook his head. At this moment he needed to follow the steps that seemed plain. As such, his focus was on the obvious suspects. He had various townspeople discreetly keeping an eye on their movements to be sure they didn't leave town, and then the country, without his knowledge. In the meantime though, he had released the body for coffining and was awaiting instructions from Mrs. Roberts as to burial. Since he was here at the hotel he might as well get the final word from her in person.

There was a lull between his knock on the suite door and the answering by Frances Roberts. When she finally opened the door, she was rubbing ink off the fingers of her left hand.

"Good afternoon, Mrs. Roberts. I'm sorry to intrude."

"As long as you don't come with handcuffs you'll be no trouble." She stepped aside for him to come into the suite.

"Right. I won't be a moment. I only wanted to know your decision as to burial."

"He can be buried here. He had no family that I ever knew about. My family is scattered across the country." Here she nodded her head towards the desk where she had apparently been writing to family members.

"Right. What about a service?"

"Just a few words at the graveside. He wasn't a man of faith. He wouldn't have wanted any fuss."

"Right. I'll send one of our pastors around to you just to get the basics."

"Fine. Am I essentially under house arrest?"

"Not at all. It's the town I'm not wanting you to leave until we can get this sorted."

She opened the door she had just closed saying, "Thank you, Chief Goodman. I must get back to my letters."

"Right."

Cool as a cucumber, he thought as he heard the door click closed behind him.

It was with some surprise that he encountered Elspeth at the station. He had supposed her to be at the hotel. Nelson Jr. was behind the counter shuffling papers not sure what to do with his guest. The police station was perfectly square but not large with a counter along the left wall when entering the door, a waiting area to the right with three beech stick chairs hard by one another and along the right wall loomed the lone cell—very rarely used. The back wall of the cell was plastered with pictures of winsome cows cast off from the local dairy's calendar. Elspeth had been intently studying these bovine beauties.

Chief Goodman's office was at the back of the station. It was essentially a transparent office as the door was all glass, with a green blind curled at the top to pull down in case of needed privacy, supported on either side by walls that were glass on the top half and sturdy oak on the bottom half. Inside, behind the metal desk, teetered the chief's wheeled, oak chair while in front stood a beech stick chair, companion to the three in the waiting area. A third chair, a cast off armchair from the Goodman home, nestled in one corner and a filing cabinet filled another. The top of the filing cabinet was home to several mugs (clean and otherwise), various keys, a pipe stand complete with pipes and a pouch of tobacco and a scattered assortment of change and nuts and bolts and nails.

Having escorted the obviously nervous Miss Roberts to the visitor's chair in his office, Chief Goodman settled himself behind his desk and picked up a pencil.

"How can I help you, Miss Roberts?"

Faced squarely with the authority that Chief Goodman represented, Elspeth seriously considered her position. What could she say? I don't want to live with my mother because I suspect her of murdering my father? And even if she did suspect her, did she really want to draw her suspicions to the attention of the police? If it turned out that her mother was guilty, Elspeth didn't think that she wanted to be the one to have offered up the evidence—such as it was.

Elspeth fingered her pearl bangles and replied, "I was just wanting to thank you for not making us feel like criminals."

"Right. Well..." he was at a loss as to what to say as it was evident that one of them had to be the criminal. He rubbed his bald head and continued, "Well, we'll be as discreet as possible. But ...while you're here I'd like to ask you some questions."

Elspeth stiffened.

"When you found your father, what did you do?" He was taking a stab in the dark here. He didn't actually know she had found him.

"I, I think I fainted."

"I see. What time did you find him?"

"I don't know."

"You must have some idea."

"Umm ... I think it might have been about 5:30."

"And when you came to what did you do?"

"Came to? Oh, I see. Um. I think I held my father's hand and cried."

"I can understand that. And then you wiped away blood stains?"

Elspeth sat ramrod straight and stared at him. Chief Goodman slowly rolled the pencil between his hands and waited.

"I ...." Long pause.

"You have a right to legal counsel, Miss Roberts. Would you like me to arrange that for you?"

Elspeth gulped and nodded.

After the meeting with Miss Roberts and Dalton Ames, the lawyer, he wrote a note to Dorothea relaying the conversation about Bill Wainfleet. He sealed it firmly and told Nelson Jr. to put it directly into Mrs. Montgomery's hand.

Chapter Nine

Elva grimly contemplated her dinner plate. Nelson Jr. had stopped by to look in on Joe and had leaked out that Elspeth was being interviewed by Chief Goodman under legal counsel. Why on earth would that be? What could Elspeth have to do with the death of her father? She wished that Joe would get better faster. Today's meeting with the chief had worn him out but she wanted to talk to him! She glanced at her ring finger where her engagement ring—wasn't. Maybe she should take George into her confidence. That was, after all, where he was supposed to be. She didn't think she wanted him to come here though because that would feel too … conciliatory. Perhaps they could meet at the Montgomerys'.

"Mother, thank you for supper. I need to make a phone call. Please excuse me."

"Yes, of course, dear," came the absent-minded reply.

Her mother had always been particular about mealtimes not being rushed but since Joe's accident she had put meals on the table but her mind was elsewhere. Her father was on the evening shift at the mill so there was no one else to hear her on the phone.

By the time the operator put her call through to The Imperial and The Imperial put it through to George's room she was beginning to waver.

"Evening," came the voice that she really did love.

"Oh, hello, George, it's Elva."

"Elva! What … are you all right?"

"Of course. I wondered if I could meet you at Mr. and Mrs. Montgomery's later this evening. I have to check with them but I wanted to know first if you could come."

"Indeed I can."

"Good," she said briskly. "I'll ring you after I speak with …"

"Aunt Dorothea," broke in George.

"Mrs. Montgomery."

A slight sigh on the other end.

"Right-ho. I'll be waiting."

Dorothea was passing through the hall when the phone rang. She sat down on the chair beside the phone table for ease of speaking into the mouthpiece.

"Montgomery residence,"

"Hello, Mrs. Montgomery, this is Elva. How are you?"

"Hello, Elva. I am well. How are you?"

"Very well too, thank you. I, I have a strange request. Um, I was hoping to use your house to, for a place to meet with George. I just need his advice about something."

"Certainly. We're here all evening so come anytime."

"Hmmm," murmured Dorothea as she replaced the receiver into its cradle.

It was Charles who had suggested making the morning room available to the young people. After all, he had said, with some of the windows facing westward a sunset would be glowing in the background and certainly sunsets have their place in romantic encounters. "It couldn't hurt," he said with a shrug. So here they were, uncertainly looking at each other, their faces tinged with rosy hues.

"I would have brought this up with Joe," began Elva, "but, of course, he isn't well enough yet. It's about Elspeth. And I do thank you for being so faithful to check in on Joe. Elspeth was questioned by the chief this afternoon. I want to help her in some way but I don't know how. I'm sure that your talking with Joe helped him. It's just that I know something that the police don't know and I'm not sure if it means anything."

"You're welcome. About Joe. What do you know?"

"Do you remember that there was a military fellow staying at The Imperial?"

George nodded.

"At first, he sort of snubbed Elspeth, apparently because she was American. But he was so absent minded that after being in the lounge or the restaurant he would leave a pen or sheet of paper or his hat or anything and it was Elspeth who always returned the items. Each time their chats became longer and longer and before she knew it, she was head over heels for him and he was the same. Whirlwind romance. Mr. Roberts wasn't at all happy about it. Something about being scornful of the Canadian military Elspeth said."

"But the military fellow left."

"Yes. And then he came back."

"He came back? When? Where is he?"

"He works at North's Bakery. He just started."

Elva touched her forehead as if to assist in the translation of her knowledge to George.

George blinked at her. "North's Bakery," he repeated slowly. "The new employee!"

Elva nodded.

"Nat, what's-his-name."

"Thompson."

George whistled. "He came back to get her?"

"That's what she thought as soon as she saw him. Although it took her a moment to recognize him because he's in disguise. He darkened his hair, began growing a moustache and put on spectacles. But, the disguise aside, she says he's acting strangely."

"What made him leave in the first place?"

"I never thought of asking that!"

"Had they planned for him to come back for her?"

"Yes. They were going to elope."

"So the disguise is to help with that?"

"Elspeth says they had never talked about a disguise."

"Seems like overkill. Surely, he could dodge Mr. Roberts without it. Why would he take a job in town if he didn't mean to stay long?"

"That's what I thought."

George stood up. "I think we should talk this over with Aunt Dot. She's good at this kind of thing."

"So, Nat Thompson is actually ... did you tell me his name?" asked Dorothea after Elva and George told her all they knew.

"Thomas Nathaniels," replied Elva.

"T.N.," said Dorothea to herself. "And you say that Chief Goodman was questioning Elspeth."

Elva nodded.

"How has Elspeth seemed to you since her father died?"

"In shock."

"Of course."

"But, she also seems skittish. It's strange."

"It's possible that your friend may be in some trouble, if—and you do need to consider this—if, she isn't after all her father's killer."

"Aunt Dot! Surely not!" said George.

"Oh dear," said Elva. "I just—I just can't see Elspeth doing such a thing. I mean if she had been planning … something, I think she would have seemed restless or furtive beforehand but she wasn't."

"There is the possibility that it was an accident," proposed George almost apologetically.

"But if it was accidental, why not just say so?" asked Dorothea. "Only someone with a guilty conscience hides something accidental."

Elva and George considered this woefully.

"What do you mean that Elspeth might be in some trouble separate from the possibility of her killing her father?" asked Elva.

"If she didn't kill her father she might know who did. She might be shielding that person."

"You mean her mother?"

"Her mother is certainly a likely suspect."

George had been watching Dorothea closely. "You think she's shielding this Nat or Thomas fellow."

Dorothea nodded.

"I know you want to help your friend, Elva dear, but it really is best to let Chief Goodman take care of it," replied Dorothea. "It seems clear that it's more than a case of young lovers plotting an elopement."

Charles, who had just entered the room with a tray of pie and coffee, said, "Now that's the pot calling the kettle black—telling these two to let the chief take care of things."

"Never mind, Charles. I know of what I speak," she said, tilting her head. "I'll have to let Chief Goodman know about this. Regrettably it fits in with some evidence."

"Oh dear. Have I made a mess of things?" asked Elva.

"The truth never makes a mess of things," said Dorothea, gently touching her hand.

Chapter Ten

After church the following morning, Dorothea sought out Chief Goodman.

"Good morning, Nelson. I'm sorry to take up your Sunday with crime but I have information pertinent to Mr. Roberts' case."

"Good. I'll take anything you've got. It wouldn't happen to explain why Bill was away from the station on Thursday would it?"

"Sadly no."

"Too bad. How 'bout I come round after dinner?"

"Fine. Our grandchildren will be arriving about then but Charles is already planning to take them out to the Brown farm to gather straw for making grass skirts."

"Right," he said, unfazed at the mention of grass skirts. "The Reverend Watkins tells me Mrs. Roberts has planned to have Mr. Roberts buried tomorrow."

Dorothea looked over to where said reverend was shaking hands with adults and bending down to peer at Sunday School artwork.

"He'll handle it wisely," she said.

"Yep. A mighty awkward situation."

"Oh, and would you mind bringing that Vermont sheet with you? I'd like to mull it over a bit."

"Right."

Sunday dinner was always a roast. On Saturday, Mrs. White arranged the veggies and meat in a roasting pan and left it in the icebox. Early Sunday morning Dorothea transferred the pan from the icebox into the warmed oven. By the time she and Charles, and any guests they may have invited, arrived back from the church service, its seductive redolence was irresistible. The one pot meal meant clean-up was basic and this Sunday she and Charles had put away the last dish with plenty of time to spare before the onslaught of grandchildren and the sober meeting with the chief.

As it turned out, everyone arrived at the same time. After Dorothea extricated herself from hugs and greetings, she waved off her daughter and son-in-law who were heading out for a Sunday afternoon drive and Charles corralled the four Little 'Uns into his car for the straw gathering expedition. Then she and the chief settled in the sitting room.

"I might as well tell you right off what Joe told me," began the chief. "The night you found Joe on the tracks he had seen a fellow in a military uniform ride off on Bill Wainfleet's bike. He yelled out and started after him but tripped and hit his head on a rock."

"Oh no," said Dorothea. "Joe is certain?"

"Certain sure. So now I've got to find where this military gent has got to. It has to be that fellow who was staying at The Imperial. I looked up his name in the registry and it's ..."

"Thomas Nathaniels."

"Now how did you know that?"

"That's what I wanted to tell you. Thomas Nathaniels is Nat Thompson, Ambrose North's new employee."

"What?"

Dorothea outlined the relationship between Elspeth and Thomas and the apparent reason for his return to Willowsdown as Nat.

"But," she continued, "what doesn't make things look good for Elspeth is the handkerchief she wanted to keep. The one with the initials T.N., presumably for

Thomas Nathaniels and the obviously washed out bloodstains."

Chief Goodman rubbed his bald head saying, "All right, so here's what Elspeth told me and Dalton Ames. She's the one who wiped the bloodstains off the wall and scrubbed them out of the carpet. She used the towel that we found in the hamper."

"And some blood must have smeared on her sleeve because there was the dress hanging in the bathroom with a damp cuff."

"Yep. The "T.N." handkerchief was on her person so that's what she started with and then ended up getting the towel. She's adamant that she didn't kill Mr. Roberts. She absolutely refuses to tell me who she thinks might want her father dead."

"It's entirely plausible that she didn't kill him and only found him."

"Yep. But if she didn't kill him, she's got something in her head about ... something."

"When Elva and George told me about Elspeth and Thomas, it occurred to me that Elspeth is shielding him. Does she know he stole the bike? But why would he steal it and then leave it at the neighbours? And yet what does that have to do with Mr. Roberts' death?"

"Did she see him around the hotel just about the time that Roberts would have been done in?"

"Maybe. She's going to have to be made aware that you know that Thomas and Nat are one and the same."

The chief nodded.

"What about Nat?"

"Don't want him to bolt. I'll talk to him before letting Miss Roberts in on what I know. Surely, the young man didn't kill Mr. Roberts because Mr. Roberts didn't like the idea of Miss Roberts walking out with him."

"It isn't likely."

"His only connection with Mr. Roberts, that we know of, is the daughter."

"So, you don't think Nat is the killer."

"I doubt it. If they were already planning to elope, he hardly needed to get the old man out of the way. Mind you, I still don't get why he came back in disguise if he was just coming for Miss Roberts." He shook his head.

"That is perplexing," agreed Dorothea.

"I'll keep checking everything I can. Someone, somewhere must have some cold hard facts."

Chief Goodman was lying on the couch in the kitchen. The Goodman home was an old farmhouse, the last building of what had been a farm in his wife's family. The farm land had been gradually sold off and the town had seeped closer so that the property was now considered just on the outskirts. Stretched out on this couch, the chief did his best thinking while the family chatter rose and fell in the background. He was forming his questions for Thomas Nathaniels.

"I feel like I spend half my day slicing bread," said Mrs. Goodman to daughter Nellie. "Here I am again slicing it for this evening's hot sandwiches. And when I'm not using the knife, I'm sharpening it."

"You know, Mom, if you think of your time as money you would actually be saving money buying sliced bread from the bakery."

Mrs. Goodman stopped mid-slice. "My time as money?"

"Yes. I get paid at the bakery for much of what you do here. By buying the bakery bread already sliced, you'll have saved all that time of making it, baking it and slicing it. Time you could be using for," Nellie said with a shrug. "I don't know—other things."

Mrs. Goodman was taken with the concept of her time being worth money.

"Well, my girl, you might have a notion there."

"Nat was saying the other day …"

Something in the tone of her daughter's voice interrupted her resumption of bread slicing. She may not understand new-fangled ideas about time and money, but she did know the sound of starry eyes.

"Now don't you be getting distracted at work by a young man," she began.

Chief Goodman prided himself on being able to think and listen at the same time. While the conversation involved bread, he could let it scatter around him and still make headway with his questioning plan. But not now. He sat bolt upright.

"Nat's not the fellow for you, Nellie. Keep your mind on your work."

The firmness in the chief's statement startled mother and daughter. He was always a gentle, easygoing father.

Walking to the table where Nellie sat, he lay his hand on her head. "Are you hearing me, my girl?" he asked, sounding like himself. "Trust your old dad."

Nellie placed her hand on top of his. "All right, Dad."

"I was going to wait 'til after supper, Mary, but on reflection, I've got police work that best not be put off."

"Well, it'll be waiting for you whenever you get back."

"I know. Thank God, for my Mary," he grinned as he slapped his wool cap on.

Chief Goodman settled himself behind his desk at the police station. He had placed a call to Thomas Nathaniels at The Imperial and arranged for him to come by the station. The chief doodled while he waited and had almost completed a sketch of the house that he and Mary kept saying they'd like to build when Thomas arrived.

"Thank you for coming," he said, motioning Thomas to the chair in front of the desk. "Now, I understand, Mr. Thompson, this town is not new to you."

"Well, I just arrived on Thursday. I'm not sure I know what you mean."

"I mean that the job you're doing at North's Bakery may be new but you've been here before."

No answer.

"In fact, you stayed at The Imperial but under the name of Thomas Nathaniels, a military fellow. I suppose the question could be asked, which is the real you? Thomas Nathaniels or Nat Thompson?"

No answer.

"As Thomas Nathaniels, you were seen, by my sergeant, this past Wednesday evening apparently stealing the bicycle of Bill Wainfleet. That was recovered so I can't charge you with the theft but I still don't know who entered the Wainfleet home uninvited. I'm thinking it was you being as you were confirmed in the area."

No answer.

"Why the disguise?"

Still no answer.

"Mr. Nathaniels, I can easily confirm your identity as a member of the armed forces as well, I imagine, as the reason you were staying at the hotel but it would be easier if you would just tell me."

No answer.

"I understand you were planning to elope with Miss Roberts."

"Miss Roberts has nothing to do with this."

"What is 'this'?"

Still no answer. He felt like sighing but that never came off professionally.

The phone jangled and both men jumped slightly.

"Police station. Chief Goodman."

"Oh, Chief, I'm glad I caught you. Mrs. Goodman said you would be there."

"How can I help you, Mrs. Quayle?"

"I was just having a chat with Dorothea, this and that about the week's doings you know and naturally the awful event of Mr. Roberts' death came up. I was telling her about being at The Imperial that afternoon and she said to me, 'Edwina, you let Chief Goodman know this right away. There are no details too trivial when it comes to a murder investigation.'"

"She's right. And the details?"

"I was at The Imperial late in the afternoon. I don't need to tell you all the ins and outs about why I was there, do I?"

"Probably not," said the chief patiently.

"Good then I'll get to the point. I saw Mr. North's new employee there. I, of course, didn't know he was anyone from town until I saw him the next day at the bakery."

"What time was that?"

"Oh, a bit after 5:00 p.m. I would say."

"I see. Where was he?"

"That's just the thing. He was in the hallway near the Roberts' suite."

He willed his eyes not to look at Thomas Nathaniels.

"Anything else?"

"At the time I thought he seemed, well, flustered or disoriented maybe. Which is normal in a stranger so I asked him if he needed help finding anything. He said he didn't and that was that."

"I see. Thank you. I'm glad you called."

"Oh good."

"If you think of anything else be sure to let me know."

"I certainly will. Well, goodbye for now, Chief Goodman. Have a pleasant evening."

He slowly hung up the receiver and moved the phone to another place on his desk in order to give himself a few extra seconds to gather his thoughts.

"I can't charge you with theft," he began," although you were seen on the bike. I can put you at the scene of a break and enter but then I have no irrefutable evidence it was you but I can, with an eyewitness, put you at the scene of Mr. Roberts' murder."

"Who says so?" asked Thomas in a strangled voice.

"Were you at The Imperial at the Roberts' suite this past Thursday sometime after 5:00 p.m.?"

No answer.

This time he did sigh. "Mr. Nathaniels, if you don't co-operate, I'll charge you with obstructing justice. For a start. Murder will likely be next. If you didn't do it and your hands are clean just give me something to work with."

Nothing.

Chief Goodman rose from his chair, took the cell key down from where it hung on a peg on the wall, paced the few steps to Thomas Nathaniels and with his hand on his shoulder said," Thomas Nathaniels, I arrest you for obstructing justice in a case of break and enter and a case of murder. I wish to give you the following warning: you need not say anything. You have nothing to hope from any promise or favour and nothing to fear from any threat whether or not you say anything. Anything you do or say may be used as evidence. Do you understand?"

Thomas Nathaniels stood. "Yes, sir, I understand."

"Come this way then."

Chapter Eleven

Early Monday morning found Dorothea strolling along the path beside the river that wound around the town. Willow trees hovered along the edge of the river for quite a stretch. She reached out to set some branches swaying murmuring, "Wind silvered willows hedge the stream..." Pacing further along, she quoted, "...still works the hidden power after a thousand springs—the medicine for heartache that lurks in lovely things." She hoped that whichever of the Roberts women who had not killed Mr. Roberts would have lovely things help with her heartache. The funeral for Mr. Roberts was scheduled for 11:00 a.m. Dorothea knew she should go. It was only respectful and kind. But her electric refrigerator was coming that morning! Even now she knew that Dilman and his young sidekick were hefting out the ice box to make room for the refrigerator. It wasn't as though she knew the Roberts. They were only passing through. And really how much respect does one show a murderer? To be able to simply plug something in that would keep food cold without heaving around chunks of ice was a thing to be celebrated! The refrigerator would change their lives. But then, she supposed, the lives of the Roberts women had been changed in a way that had no going back. She sighed. One of them had apparently been affected in such a desperate way as to take drastic action.

Ahead of her, the river narrowed substantially and a bridge connected one side of the town to the other. In the middle of the bridge, a woman leaned against the railing looking down the river away from Dorothea. It always amazed her how people can be recognized just by their backs. This woman she did not recognize. And as such she concluded that she likely knew who it was. The question was, did she continue on her walking loop which meant crossing the bridge or did she turn back and retrace her steps? She slowed her steps as she passed another willow tree and peered through the lace of the trailing branches. There was no one else around on either side of the river. Squaring her shoulders, Dorothea quickened her pace as she approached the bridge. She had taken several steps onto the wooden planks before Mrs. Roberts was aware of her and slightly turned her head. Mrs. Roberts' face was set but tears shimmered in her eyes.

Innocent until proven guilty, thought Dorothea. "I'm sorry that your visit to our town ends this way," she said.

Mrs. Roberts turned back to the river. "So am I."

Dorothea stood uncertainly and then said, "I will see you later this morning."

Mrs. Roberts just acknowledged this with a minimal lift of a hand.

Well! thought Dorothea, *the celebration of the refrigerator would have to wait. Nothing would keep her from the funeral now. Scrutiny of Mrs. Roberts was the thing.*

Thankfully, although the May morning was cool it was sunny. Graveside meetings are no fun at any time but are particularly miserable in the midst of rotten weather. There hadn't been a funeral service at either a church or the funeral home; Mrs. Roberts had requested that only the graveside order of service be said.

When Dorothea and Charles arrived, the only other people besides Frances and Elspeth Roberts and Reverend Watkins (and, of course, the grave diggers who were standing respectfully at a distance) were Elva North, George Seyler, Mr. Schlessinger, the hotel manager, Muriel Brown and Ambrose North. It wasn't long though until Chief Goodman appeared and Anna Wainfleet, Edwina and Edwin Quayle, various church members, a few guests from the hotel and finally Mrs. Johnson who puffingly whispered to Dorothea that she needn't be disquieted imagining that the store was left unattended as Mr. Johnson decided to forgo attending the burial in order to maintain retail order. Thus relieved, Dorothea attended to the scene before her.

"This is a sad occasion and I'm glad to see that our visitors do not stand here alone," began Reverend Watkins, his white hair and beard bright in the spring sunlight. "Death is a great leveler as no one is exempt. It is a reminder that we all share the same fate. That we are all made from the same substance—that we all share this truth: we didn't decide when and how our lives began and neither do we decide when and how they will end. But in the middle, we can decide to whom we will belong. With such lack of control over such decisive parts of our lives we obviously can't belong just to ourselves. No one is outside the redeeming love of God and we are welcome to take His name at any time."

He paused and Dorothea who had positioned herself so that she could discreetly examine Mrs. Roberts throughout the service without being noticed (hopefully), saw that although Elspeth was crying and clasping and unclasping her gloved hands, Mrs. Roberts continued with an expressionless face. It occurred to Dorothea that both women were outfitted entirely in black and not ill-fitting clothes as might be the case when mourning clothes had to be borrowed or purchased in not quite the right size. Were they able to put such smart outfits together in the few days since

Mr. Roberts' death? She would have to check in at the town's ladies' dress shop. Or did they come equipped? In that case it was more likely Mrs. Roberts who had killed her husband because it wouldn't seem strange for her to suggest packing mourning clothes—just in case— —as it would be for a young woman like Elspeth to do so.

Reverend Watkins was speaking out the familiar passage from Psalm 103 and Dorothea closed her eyes as she loved hearing the words.

"Like as a father pities his own children even so is the Lord merciful unto them that fear Him. For He knows whereof we are made. He remembers that we are but dust. The days of man are but as grass for he flourishes as a flower of the field. For as soon as the wind goes over it, it is gone and the place thereof shall know it no more. But the merciful goodness of the Lord endures for ever and ever upon them that fear Him and his righteousness upon children's children."

The reverend nodded to Mrs. and Miss Roberts who stepped forward and each scooping a handful of dirt from the pile by the grave dropped their handfuls onto the coffin.

"We commend unto thy hands of mercy, most merciful Father, the soul of this our brother departed, and we commit his body to the ground, earth to earth, ashes to ashes, dust to dust. And we beseech thine infinite goodness to give us grace to live in thy fear and love and to die in thy favour, that when the judgement shall come which thou hast committed to thy well-beloved Son, both this our brother and we may be found acceptable in thy sight. Grant this, O merciful Father, for the sake of Jesus Christ, our only Saviour, Mediator, and Advocate."

"Amen," said all those around the grave.

What Reverend Watkins did next afforded many tongues satisfying food for comment for quite some time after. Tucking his service book under his arm, he walked around the grave to where the Roberts' women stood and placed a hand on each of their shoulders saying, "I bless you in the name of Jesus, that he might be your comforter and that you may feel the comfort and sustenance of God in your waking and sleeping, working and playing." Then he lowered his voice which was a signal that everyone was to mind their own business as he continued talking with them.

Dorothea had heard Mrs. Johnson's intake of breath so was expecting it when that worthy woman exclaimed, "Imagine! A blessing! And one of them the man's killer! But then as he said we can all make a choice of belonging at any time. My, my."

The small funeral group splintered into smaller clusters. Dorothea remained where she was and unintentionally began tuning into the conversation taking place amongst the circle of the hotel guests.

"...and really what other conclusion can be drawn? She seems not to mind leaving her husband buried in a foreign land. She obviously doesn't care that she can't visit his grave. That seems cold-hearted."

Dorothea moved away so as not to be eavesdropping and shook hands with Reverend Watkins who was watching the retreating Roberts' women. She said, "Blessing not cursing, well done."

"An awkward situation. Seemed right to offer hope. And now I suppose you'll be wanting me to tell you my impressions of Chief Goodman's suspects?" he teased.

"Well ..." said Dorothea, tilting her head, "You've known many people over the years...."

"Yes, and so I would say that they both are hiding something. Can't be of more help than that."

"They did it together?"

"I'll leave that to you and the chief."

Chief Goodman was shifting from foot to foot as he listened to an earnest recital from Mrs. Johnson. Muriel Brown came up beside Dorothea and, following Dorothea's gaze, said, "I imagine she's telling him about how she saw Mr. Roberts and Alex Kaminen in conversation in front of the store on Wednesday evening."

"Really? I didn't know Alex knew the Roberts."

Mrs. Brown shrugged. "He likely didn't. Just some random exchange."

"How do you know about it?"

"Mrs. Johnson mentioned it to me."

"And did she say how they seemed with each other? Was the conversation friendly or serious or ..." Dorothea trailed off.

"Well, you know Mrs. Johnson." Both women smiled. "But she said, hmm let me see something like ... conferencing, that was the word!"

"Conferencing. That doesn't help much."

"I suppose not." And like any good farmer, Mrs. Brown turned the conversation to the things of this world and asked, "How did the straw work out for the grass skirts?"

Dorothea and Charles were walking home with Edwina and Edwin. Crossing the town's larger bridge, they all stopped to lean over and watch the water flow under. It swooped by as if singing for gladness that it carried only itself and not also winter's debris. Still pondering the various moments of the funeral, Dorothea had only been partially listening to Edwina's conversation until Edwina, wrapping up a statement, said, "You never know with Americans. They always seem to be worked up about something. And, apparently still wanting to annex us. You'd think the

War of 1812 would've settled all that. Never mind this last war where we pulled our weight long before they did."

Dorothea wasn't quite sure she could follow the logic of all this but she asked, "Edwin, you travel to the States, do you hear talk of annexation?"

Edwin smiled fondly at his wife and replied, "Of course not. Edwina's imagination is great for books but perhaps not a reflection of common current events."

"Hmph," said Edwina as the foursome continued over the bridge where they parted ways.

"You're very quiet," remarked Charles after they had walked through the downtown without any comment from Dorothea."

"Yes," she agreed.

"What's on your mind?"

"I'm not quite sure. There's something I know that I can't remember but that I'm sure connects something with something."

"Ah."

"You can see why I'm not saying anything; I've nothing of intelligence to say but I know there's a fact elusively floating around in my head."

"You'll catch it."

She smiled at him. "Just think! When we get home, there'll be an electric refrigerator!"

Behind his desk at the police station, Chief Goodman was plunking away on the typewriter. Nat Thompson had given him the name of his superior officer, Colonel James Sutherland Brown, and the chief was typing a letter requesting information about his jailbird.

He had stopped by The Imperial after the funeral. In light of Mrs. Johnson's account of the conversation between Mr. Roberts and Alex Kaminen, he interviewed hotel staff as to whether or not they had seen Alex Kaminen anywhere near the Roberts' suite. No one had. Mrs. Johnson described the conversation between the two men as agitated. She admitted she couldn't hear them as she was in the store window and they were outside, but she said their faces and hand gestures indicated an unhappy exchange. The only people who had seen Alex at the hotel were the kitchen staff but that was normal as that was the day for the meat delivery. He still needed to speak with the young fellow who had taken over Alex's delivery route while Alex was visiting his mother. He'd get to that in good time. What needed to happen after he dropped this letter in the mailbox was to ask Mrs. Roberts if she knew Alex. When he questioned the hotel staff earlier, he hadn't wanted to intrude upon Mrs. Roberts so soon after the funeral but it had to be done yet that afternoon.

Chief Goodman tugged the letter out of the typewriter and glanced towards the cell. He had asked Nelson Jr. to fingerprint Nat. The two young men sat on the cell cot with the fingerprinting apparatus between them. The cell door was swung wide open. The chief sighed. He hoped they'd never have any desperate criminals in their keep. With "one eye" on the fingerprinting proceedings, a quick rummage in his desk produced an envelope. He'd get a stamp at the post office. At the same moment that the chief walked out of his office and Nelson Jr. locked the cell door, the station door slowly opened. It was Elspeth.

Nat rose from his cot and the two of them stared at each other.

Chief Goodman cleared his throat. "Right, Junior, I'm off. Just heading to the post office. You hold down the fort."

"Ah, would you like a chair, miss?" asked Nelson.

"No, I don't think I'll be long."

Behind the counter, Nelson Jr. was rustling papers and whatever he could find as loudly as he could but he needn't have bothered. The suspects, one on each side of the bars, weren't saying anything. Finally, while he was making a clattering with the metal coffee pot on the potbellied stove, Elspeth let out a sob and ran out of the station. The two young fellows looked blankly at each other as the door banged.

"Do you want a cup of coffee?" asked Junior holding up the pot.

Nat slumped back onto his cot. "Yeah. And if you had anything stronger, I'd take that too."

Mrs. Roberts was holding a glass clinking with ice cubes when she answered the door. From the whiff he caught, Chief Goodman knew it wasn't lemonade. *Well, I can't be all things to all people*, he thought. *I can't be the prohibition police right now. And anyway, the liquid might loosen her tongue.*

"I have a few questions for you."

"I thought as much."

"I'm sorry to have to trouble you so soon after your husband's funeral."

"Sooner or later doesn't make him any less dead."

"True. Thanks," he said as she waved him to a rounded charcoal grey chair.

"How well did you and your husband know Alex Kaminen?"

"Alex Kaminen? Who on earth is he?"

"He's a resident of Willowsdown. He works at the butcher shop. Your husband was seen in conversation with him."

Mrs. Roberts shrugged. "I never heard of him."

"Where do you live, Mrs. Roberts?"

"Grand Portage, Minnesota."

"Just over the border then."

Mrs. Roberts nodded and sipped.

"Was your husband, by any chance, involved in a business that brought him into Canada?"

"Yes."

"And that business was...?"

"He was in the lumber business."

"So he visited lumber mills on a regular basis?"

"Yes."

"I see. Would he have done business in Port Arthur by any chance?"

"I have no idea. There was a time when I travelled with my husband—when we didn't want to be apart. But that hasn't been the case for a number of years. I haven't been keeping track of his business travels."

"Did your daughter travel with him?"

"She did when I used to travel with him."

"But not lately?"

"No. But she was very fond of her father. She adored him."

"I see."

"I, however, did not."

"You were out for a walk in the late afternoon on Thursday but before that you had tea with your husband and daughter in the restaurant at The Imperial. You were overheard to say to your husband," Chief Goodman rifled through the pages of his pad, 'I'm done with this and I'm going to stop you. I don't know how but I will.'"

"My, my, what big ears someone has. Yes, I did say that. Robert was being nonsensical about Elspeth and the young man she was sweet on."

"Thomas Nathaniels—the military fellow who was staying at the hotel at the time."

Mrs. Roberts raised her glass as if in toast. "Well done. You are rightly informed." She continued to meet his gaze squarely.

"So far no one has come forward to say they saw you out walking when you claim that you were."

She shrugged again. "Well, I was."

Chief Goodman flapped his pad shut. "I'm sure I don't need to remind you but I will anyway—don't leave town."

"I have no intention of doing so," she replied calmly.

On the way back to the station, Chief Goodman stopped in at the bakery to pick up a pie. He knew he could do with some pie and coffee and likely Junior could too. And Thomas/Nat too.

"I have a bone to pick with you," said Ambrose North coming out of the kitchen, wiping his hands on his apron. "You've got my new employee behind bars and he was shaping up as a great asset here. I'm getting too old for this up-at-the-crack-of-dawn-to-set-the-bread-to-rise work. What do you have him in for anyway? The lad just got into town."

"Sorry, Ambrose, but I'm going to be official and say no comment as it's police business."

Mr. North sighed. "Well, I think you're barking up the wrong tree, however, I'm sure you know your business. What can I do for you?"

"I've got a hankering for pie. What do you suggest?"

"There's a rhubarb one but your Nellie pulled out a blueberry pie not long ago. Made from last summer's berries that we froze."

"Blueberry would be great." On a hunch he asked, "Did you happen to send Thom .., ah Nat, to The Imperial on a delivery last Thursday?"

Mr. North screwed up his mouth as he considered. Nellie popped her head around the kitchen door and said, "Yes, you did. Remember? They called at the last moment to see if we had any raisin bread left; they wanted it to make French toast the next morning."

"Right you are."

"Do you know what time that might have been?"

"What do you think, Nellie? It would have been after 5:00...."

Chief Goodman could tell that his daughter, having realized that Nat being at the hotel at that time put him in a compromised position, was reluctant to contribute but she finally said, "It was closer to 5:30."

"I see."

"Tuck that blueberry pie in a bag there, Nellie. Anything else, Chief?"

"That's it. Thanks for the sustenance."

He patted his daughter's hand as she handed him the pie. "It'll be all right, sweetheart," he said under his breath.

"Hey, Dad, uh Chief," said Nelson Jr. as the chief stepped into the station. "I've actually had two people come in to say they saw Mrs. Roberts walking on Thursday afternoon."

"How about that. Hmm. She's a hard one to read."

"And..." Nelson Jr. lowered his voice, "I've finished with the fingerprinting."

"I see. Come into my office. Grab some cutlery and plates from the shelf there on your way."

"What do you have?" asked the chief quietly as he sliced pieces from the pie.

"Thomas' prints match the print from the mantelpiece."

He looked at the third piece of pie and debated whether or not to share it.

"Have you found a print that is unidentifiable?"

"No."

"All right. Good job. Take this to Mr. Nathaniels. But first. What did Miss Roberts have to say to him?"

"Nothing. She just burst out crying and scampered."

"I see. On second thought I'll take him the pie. He'll have to explain about the fingerprint."

After the rigmarole of unlocking the cell and handing in the pie and relocking the cell and pulling up a chair for himself on the outside of the cell and realizing he couldn't eat his own pie and take notes, the chief took a seat and opened his mouth to begin his questions when Thomas blurted out, "I've been waiting for you to return. I've got something to tell you."

"Really," replied the chief dryly. "About time. It wouldn't have anything to do with fingerprints would it?"

"Fingerprints never occurred to me until they were taken," said Thomas nodding towards Nelson Jr. "What I have to say is that I did see Mr. Roberts that day. I had determined to have it out with him about Miss Roberts. To tell him that we were going to marry whether he liked it or not. But he was drunk enough that he was just rude. There was no point in trying to discuss anything with him so I left."

"Why couldn't you have told me this before?"

"I, I don't know."

"You and Mr. Roberts discussed this in his study?"

"We stood around in the living area. I guess if that was his study then yes, we met in his study."

"How did the conversation unfold?"

"I had taken off my glasses and told him who I was. I thought he would make a big deal of my disguise but he didn't. I said that Elspeth and I loved each other. We were hoping for his blessing to our marriage. He just looked at me kind of breathing heavily. I was standing in front of the mantelpiece and he walked over to me and kept coming closer until I was backed against it. I put my hand on the ledge to brace myself, I guess, because I wasn't sure what he might do. He stood about two inches from me and glared at me. Finally he said,

'You're a nobody from a nowhere country. You can forget it.' There didn't seem any point in staying so as I said I left."

"Was this when you delivered the bread to the hotel?"

"No. This was just before 5:00 p.m. When I arrived back at the bakery that was when the hotel called asking about the bread and I returned to the hotel kitchen. That was around 5:30 p.m."

"Did you see anyone in the hallway outside of the Roberts' suite?"

"Which ti… uh, no, sir. No one."

Chief Goodman held the gaze of his suspect who cleared his throat but didn't look away.

"I'm going to set your bail. Mr. North wants you back but this murder and the break in are still unfinished business."

"May I let Miss Roberts know about the bail?" Thomas asked tentatively.

The chief rubbed his head and considered. "All right," he finally said. "But eat your pie first."

Chapter Twelve

George strolled into the bakery on his afternoon break. He needed to clear his head from the smoke-filled office of insurance claims. Besides, he knew Elva's grandfather liked him. He figured all is fair in love and war and he was happy to take the help of any ally. Mr. North was behind the counter.

"Look who the cat dragged in! How are you, George?"

"Pretty fair, Mr. North. And you?"

"Not bad considering I'm down an employee. Our good chief has my new man tied up in jail—well, not literally."

"I heard something about that. So, he's still there?"

"Yep."

"Hmmm. Maybe I should take him something."

"I doubt it. Chief Goodman was in earlier and took away a pie. If I know him, he offered some to his prisoner."

George hesitated. "In case he didn't, I'll take a couple of slices of that pound cake."

"Right you are."

Mr. North shook his head as George closed the bakery door behind him and headed to the police station. "That's one well-fed prisoner," he said to himself.

"I've brought you something," said George, clutching the paper bag as he reached through the bars to shake Thomas' hand. "Some pound cake."

"Thanks, but I just had a piece of pie not long ago."

"George!" the chief called from his office. "Just step in here a moment."

Chief Goodman gently closed the office door as George sat.

"You might be able to offer Mr. Nathaniels more than cake. Would you be interested in paying his bail?"

"Thank you, Mr. Seyler," said Thomas as the two men stood on the sidewalk in front of the police station. "I'll get that money back to you by tomorrow."

"At your convenience and call me George. Where are you off to now?"

"Well…" Thomas shifted uncertainly from foot to foot. "Would you mind coming to my room? I have something to tell you that I probably should have told the chief, but—well, I'm not sure it's worth his notice."

Still holding his bag of pound cake, George said, "I'm just on my break from the office but I could come after work."

Thomas' face registered disappointment as though he feared he might lose his nerve in the intermediate hours but he said, "Let me provide you with supper and we can talk then."

They shook hands in agreement and walked their separate ways.

The Montgomery household was huddled in awe around the new electric refrigerator. The door of the refrigerator had been left open for several minutes and each household member waved his or her hand in the interior to confirm that it still held its chill.

"We should probably close the door now," said Charles who should have been at the office but wanted to see for himself the new appliance in situ.

Dianna and Mrs. White had arranged the food stuffs on the four levels inside and filled the ice trays with water. They had their own compact compartment of two shelves.

"Do you really think that water will freeze into cubes of ice?" asked Dianna.

"Well, that's what this brochure promises," said Mrs. White, waving said piece of paper.

"It better," said Dilman. "The whole point of these contraptions is not to have to haul ice every other day."

The door continued standing open as everyone gazed inside, pondering this wonder.

The saga of how to keep food chilled began every winter on Willowsdown's river. The town's iceman was Izzy Withrow, Dr. Caleb Withrow's brother. Come about January, Izzy would drill a hole into the ice on the river and slide a ruler into the hole. If the thickness of the ice measured somewhere around a foot it was ready to be harvested. He would gather a crew of farmers and they would descend on the river with a couple of ice plows and saws and picks and ice chisels and tongs and horses and wagons. Because snow slows freezing, the first task was to remove any snow. Once the ice was cleared, the horse drawn plow sliced the ice in long strips making a wide channel. These strips were sawn into blocks three or four feet long. The blocks were floated and manoeuvred to the river bank where there was a ramp leading to a wagon. The work was essential but it could be dangerous and was, of course, a day working in freezing temperatures. All these were elements that contributed to a lasting camaraderie for those who worked on the river.

Once the blocks were loaded onto the wagons, they were transported to the town's ice house. Willowsdown's ice house was a triple brick structure surrounded by tall pines and facing north. Here the blocks were stacked high and separated by sawdust. Every day throughout the year, Izzy made his route delivering blocks of ice to the town's households. Some homes had their own small ice pit where they could keep a small supply of blocks whereas others needed delivery every other day. But everyone had to lug the blocks in and out of their iceboxes.

"I wonder if the ice cubes will be as refreshing as shavings from the block?" asked Dorothea.

Everyone knew the lovely feel of shaved ice on the tongue on a hot summer's day.

Mrs. White referred again to the brochure.

"Five cubic feet!" she exclaimed.

"And," added Dianna, "it says it's healthier because it 'keeps the food consistently cool'.."

"I really think we should shut the door," Charles prompted.

"I wonder how many other people will be getting electric refrigerators?" asked Dianna.

There was a contemplative silence.

"Does that mean..." began Dorothea, "Do you think they will ever replace iceboxes? Because then Izzy would be without work. In fact, a whole way of life would be gone."

"Nope. Don't see that many people being able to afford these things," said Dilman, waving his hand again into the refrigerator's interior. "Don't worry about Izzy. We'll still be cartin' blocks until the cows come home. You aren't gettin' rid of your icebox even though you've got one of these."

Did Dorothea detect a slight tone of disgust?

Charles took matters into his hands then and shut the refrigerator door.

"I think the thing is brilliant," he said, clapping Dilman on the shoulder. "Sorry about keeping the icebox, but look at it this way. At least we got this and not another one."

"Well, all I can say is, I'll have fewer sleepless nights knowin' that there won't be any food going off!" exclaimed Mrs. White.

"And we certainly don't want you to have any sleepless nights," said Dorothea, giving her faithful employee a peck on the cheek.

After the satisfactory inspection of the new electric refrigerator, which confirmed that it continued to stay cold even as the door was open and shut, Dorothea headed downtown to the ladies' dress shop under the pretext of looking for dresses for her granddaughters. She and the owner, Miss Ernst, chatted happily about the new batch of outfits that had recently come in for summer wear. Dorothea directed the conversation to the comfort of well-fitting clothes. From there, she commented on how nicely outfitted the Roberts' women were at the funeral.

"You did well to have what they needed on such short notice," she remarked.

"Yes, that doesn't always happen. I had in stock all they wanted in just the right sizes. Considering the shocking situation they're in, I was glad that the funeral clothes came together so easily for them. Such a terrible accident."

Dorothea was glad to hear that Miss Ernst at least was still under the impression that Mr. Roberts had died accidentally, although, by now she must be among only a few. Apparently, and unaccountably, she must not have been in conversation with Mrs. Johnson over the last number of days. Regardless of Miss Ernst's understanding of the situation, what was clear was that Frances and Elspeth Roberts had not come prepared for a funeral. And that had to mean something.

The Imperial offered a variety of rooms. There were a few suites. One, of course, was closed off as part of the ongoing police investigation and another was occupied by Mrs. and Miss Roberts. Another was the temporary home of George. And then there were a few rooms more like tiny apartments with limited but adequate means to prepare simple meals. In one such had Thomas Nathaniels taken up residence. It was difficult to concentrate with criminal charges over one's head but the kitchen was one place he wasn't forgetful or clumsy. He'd always enjoyed helping his mother prepare meals and baked goods—most of all baked goods. His father though insisted on a military career. It astonished him, actually, to think how far he had come given his propensity to forget things or drop files. But he had an eye for detail, which works well in the kitchen and in the long run had worked well for him in the career he had landed in. After departing from George, he had assured Mr. North that he would be back at work the following day. From there, he headed over to George Flesherton's butcher shop, picking up some veal cutlets to which he could give a quick fry for the evening meal. By the time George arrived after work, Thomas was ready with a meal and a confession. It took him until after-dinner coffee to spit it out—the confession, of course, not the coffee.

"I, ah, wasn't entirely straight with Chief Goodman. Well, no, I was truthful, but I didn't tell him everything."

George nodded. "'…sinned against You by what we have left undone' or unsaid as in this case."

"Yes, exactly. Chief Goodman asked me if I had seen anyone near the Roberts' suite and I said I hadn't."

"But …"

"But, well, I did." He gulped some coffee. "I saw Elspeth," he said faintly.

"She does live there," pointed out George. "When was it that you saw her?"

"When I went back to take some bread to the kitchen. She didn't see me. I don't know exactly why I returned to that floor—maybe a crazy thought to try and talk to Mr. Roberts again. Anyway, there she was coming out of the room. She had such a strange look on her face that I left. I don't know. I seemed to be acting as strangely as she was. Normally I would be more than happy to have a chance to talk with her."

"Did you kill Mr. Roberts?" asked George, lighting a cigarette.

"I'm a military man!" exclaimed Thomas with a hurt look.

George looked at him oddly and blew smoke out of his mouth sideways.

"Well, not that kind of military man," said Thomas.

"What kind of military man are you then? Actually, never mind that. More to the point: you can't protect Elspeth from the law. If she didn't do it then that will come out. If she did…" He shrugged. "Maybe she isn't the girl you thought she was."

Thomas slumped slightly. "If she did, she definitely isn't the girl I thought she was." He straightened up again. "But it isn't possible. It just isn't in her."

"We're all capable of pretty dastardly stuff. And, anyway, who can unravel the 'infinite variety' of woman?"

Thomas stiffened. "If you're referring to Miss North breaking off your engagement—Elspeth told me—it's hardly in the same league."

"You're right. Sorry, old chap."

The two sat silently, George smoking and Thomas fidgeting.

"There wouldn't be anything else you need to get off your chest is there?" asked George.

"No," was the short reply.

"Righty-ho. What do you want to do?"

"I think I should talk to Elspeth—if she'll talk to me."

"Look, why don't I see if Elva can get Elspeth to meet with you."

Thomas nodded slowly. "Maybe. Seeing me behind bars likely didn't help me any."

"Likely not. Let me see what I can set up. As you said, it doesn't compare, but I am walking on thin ice too so it may or may not come off."

"I'd appreciate you trying. I'll have to face Chief Goodman with this sometime soon but if we *can* meet with Elspeth first it would sit better with me."

"All right," said George, stubbing out his cigarette. "I'll let you know. Thanks for supper. Come to think of it, it was great."

They shook hands and parted for the second time that day.

As the only daughter, with four older brothers, Elva had always enjoyed the luxurious privacy of her own bedroom. She was proud of the wallpaper with its soft lavender background and rows of clustered warm purple roses bracketed with black scrolling. She had never actually seen a purple rose and doubted if such a thing existed but it seemed appropriate to cover the walls of one's bedroom with visions of what might be. She could lie in bed and look out her bedroom window. Her room didn't face directly east so when the sun rose on a clear morning the sky was just smudged with opalescence. To the left of the window was a plush boudoir chair in cream velvet. It was a new purchase and Elva smiled every time she looked at it. An old dresser was next to it—looking very shabby indeed beside the chair. And then the dressing table with three mirrors and the small cushioned bench newly covered with cream velvet. It was on that bench that Elspeth was perched.

"Elspeth, are you going to tell me what's bothering you or not?"

Since retreating to Elva's room, Elspeth had teetered on the edge of the bed, then alighted for a few minutes on the chair and now finally balanced rigidly on the edge of the bench with her hands pushing down against the velvet and causing her shoulders to hunch.

"I think so."

She edged back a bit on the bench and clasped her hands tightly together in her lap. Elva plumped up the pillow that was behind her to soften the ridges of the iron bedstead.

"It's Thomas."

Elva waited.

"I saw him coming out of our suite."

"I thought you said you saw him coming out of the hotel."

"I did say that. I wasn't ready to say that more precisely I had seen him coming out of the suite."

"So…"

"So, when I was sitting in the window at the library I saw him go into the hotel. I waited for a few minutes and then I went over. I thought we could talk. When I got there I took the elevator. He came out of the room and turned toward the stairs so he didn't see me as I stepped out. I called to him but he apparently didn't hear. He was rushing down the steps. I was going to follow him but then I realized he probably had to get back to work. I figured he would get in touch later so I just went back to the library. When I returned to our suite, there was my father—dead."

"What time was it when you saw Thomas?"

"About 5:00 p.m. A bit after I think."

"Did the elevator attendant see him?"

"Oh, I don't think so. He was behind the button panel."

"But he would have heard you call to Thomas."

"Yes. Yes he would."

"Have you told Chief Goodman this?"

Elspeth fiddled with her bangles.

"No," she finally said.

"Elspeth! Chief Goodman is bound to question the hotel staff so he *will* hear about this. If you haven't told him everything it will look very badly for you."

"I talked to the lawyer, Mr. Ames too."

"And did you tell him about Thomas?"

"No," came the faint reply.

Elva threw up her hands and slid to sit on the edge of the bed.

"If Thomas did this thing you can't screen him. He may not be all you think him to be. It's better to know that now. What if you had eloped and he turned out to be a murderer?"

Elspeth looked up revealing her misery.

"Elspeth, I'm sorry. I don't mean to be harsh. Do you see what I mean though?"

Elspeth nodded.

"But there's more. It's about my mother."

"Oh gracious. Your mother?"

"While we were having tea at The Imperial, my mother told me that she was going for a walk when we were done. My father joined us then and it became a little—ah—well, unpleasant I guess, so I left and went to the library. It's been unpleasant a lot lately. As soon as I got there I found a window seat. I wanted to be alone but not at the suite so I sort of mindlessly watched the comings and goings on main street. It wasn't until the day after my father's death that I realized that I hadn't seen my mother leave the hotel for her walk. I asked her about it and she said that she had left by the back door. But then she said that she changed her mind about her route and did pass by the library. She told me that she hadn't seen me in the window. The point is that she could have killed my father."

The two friends sat silently—one musing sorrowfully the other methodically.

"She said she hadn't seen you sitting in the window?"

"Yes."

"You do realize don't you, that it might have been her way of saying that she wonders what you were doing at that time? That if you weren't at the library, then where were you?"

Elspeth jumped up from the bench.

"No! She wouldn't!"

"You are wondering about her…"

Elspeth stood clasping and unclasping her hands together.

"This just gets worse and worse!" she groaned.

"It's an unlikely web to be sure. I know it's painful to talk about but please tell me everything—everything, Elspeth. Two heads are better than one so they say."

Elspeth slumped onto the cushioned bench.

"I don't think there's anything else to say about Thomas—or mother."

"All right, but you did go back to the suite. What time was that?"

"I think around 5:30 p.m."

"And…?"

Elspeth covered her face.

"And that's when I found him and I thought Thomas had done it. So, I scrubbed the walls and the carpet where there were spots of blood. I rinsed out the towel and handkerchief I used. The handkerchief was Thomas' I knew because it had his initials on it. The dress I was wearing got some blood smears on the cuff so I took that off and rinsed it too. I let it all hang out to dry. It seemed to me that a few damp pieces of laundry wouldn't be considered unusual. And then I left. I didn't know what to do."

"It was your mother, then, who called the police."

Elspeth nodded.

"I'm sorry to ask you this, but was there blood on your father?"

Elspeth considered. "No, not really, I don't think."

"You didn't wipe blood off of him?"

"No."

"Elspeth, let's assume that Thomas didn't do this and talk to him. Who knows? Maybe he somehow thinks you did it and you're both covering for one another. Stranger things have happened."

"I suppose. He did call to tell me he was out on bail. In fact, it was George who paid his bail."

"George did?"

"Yes."

"Oh."

"Maybe George knows something about Thomas."

"Maybe. I don't think Thomas would let you know about being released if he wanted to avoid you."

"I suppose not."

"Would it, would it help if George and I were with you and Thomas when you meet?"

"Yes. Oh yes, that would help."

"Well, I'll, um, I'll talk to George."

"Could it be soon please?"

"Of course," said Elva, warmly reaching out to squeeze one of Elspeth's clenched hands. "I'll see if I can reach George tonight."

Elspeth wanted to be alone so Elva set her up in the bedroom with a few books, a pot of tea and a handkerchief dotted with lavender drops. She, on the other hand, was bracing herself to walk over to The Imperial to call on George. As she shrugged on her coat the front door bell rang.

"I'll get it, Mom," she called.

She opened the door to find George outlined against the topaz sunset.

"Oh," she said.

The smile on his face faded and there was a slight upward tipping of his chin.

"Miss North, I've come on behalf of my friend, Thomas Nathaniels."

"You have?" She could have kissed his whole face then and there. It came back to her how, when they barely knew each other, she and Joe and George had raced each other on the town's frozen river. She hadn't won but she hadn't lost either. All three had arrived within a handbreadth of each other. He had heartily and graciously shaken her hand as an equal in the contest. And then his all-out help to Mrs. Montgomery in finding his grandmother's brooch had been so sweet and heartwarming. "I was just coming to you on behalf of my friend, Elspeth Roberts."

"You were?" He was reminded of the time she gave him a run for his money in a skating contest; her short legs against the longer legs of himself and Joe and she had swept to the finish line of his grandmother's scarf just a handbreadth behind them. And the first time he heard her reasoned thinking at a book club meeting and she taking his measure merely as a man, not as a rich man. The smile returned slowly and the two of them stood gazing serenely at each other until Elva's mother could be heard calling.

"Elva, who is it? Please close the door; there's a draft."

"Sorry, Mom," to her mother. "Please come in," to George.

Chapter Thirteen

"Mrs. Montgomery, look! Ice cubes already! This electric refrigerator works a treat," exclaimed Mrs. White, sweeping open the door when Dorothea entered the kitchen the following morning.

Dorothea peered into the freezer section of the new wonder appliance. "Well! It won't take any time to come up with ice for the ice cream maker. Dilman won't have to break up ice blocks into small enough pieces for the churn. That'll please him."

"Oh, you can be sure of that. He hates dealing with the ice blocks. Poor fellow. He'll be patting that refrigerator every time he passes it. Now, you were wanting to make a practice batch of those cookies for the Guides this morning, is that right?"

"That's right."

"Dianna got some vanilla sugar from Ambrose yesterday so I've got all the ingredients here. We can make the dough and while it's chilling, we can talk about what food you want for the rest of the weekend."

Dorothea smiled to herself. She wondered at times who employed whom.

Dorothea and Mrs. White had tackled the Girl Guide cookie baking early in the morning so the dough had been mixed, chilled, rolled out, shaped, baked, cooled and cookies were ready for testing just about the time that others might be ready for a midmorning nibble.

Dorothea decided to take a few samples around and see what people thought. She was very pleased with them but it's always good to hear from unbiased sources. She would start with Edwina, although she supposed Edwina couldn't be considered unbiased.

"Dorothea! I was just thinking of you. What do you have there?" asked Edwina eagerly after Dorothea had helloed and come in the never locked side door at her friend's house.

"These, my dear friend, are the cookies that the Guides are going to sell at the Victoria Day celebration. Here is your copy of the recipe. I'll need you to make a few dozen. I think you'll agree that they'll be a hit."

"Oho! You did a trial run. Good idea. Let's have at 'em. Oh my! They are yummy. But don't take them around to too many people. We should keep them as a surprise."

"Good point. I was thinking of taking some to Elva and Olive at the exchange office."

"Well, that would be all right. They know how to be discreet. But don't go to the Grocery Emporium."

"It never crossed my mind."

"Speaking of Mrs. Johnson, I just came back from there and she told me that George Flesherton told her that Alex Kaminen is delayed in returning to Willowsdown because his mother has finally decided to move from Port Arthur and settle here. Isn't that good news? I'm sure it's a good idea. Alex has always seemed to me to be a kind-hearted fellow—our gentle giant. It's likely been difficult knowing his mother was alone. Apparently, the loss of that mill was a double blow because it had been built up by his mother's father and his father's father. The two men—who would be Alex's grandfathers—went into business together as young men. Fancy that, eh? So, there was sentimental attachment to the business as well as financial. What with the lumber mill failing and her husband's death, why stay there when her son and sister are here? I can't imagine that kind of loss and grief. That's what I would do—come here I mean. And Joe North is up and about. Well up and about at home. I spoke with his mother at the Emporium and she's so happy. She said he's starting to be more like himself. He requested a favourite meal for supper tonight so she was there getting supplies and obviously thrilled that he was feeling well enough to eat so heartily."

"That's good to hear. Chief Goodman did arrest the military fellow but at least he doesn't seem to be guilty of an assault on Joe."

"What military fellow?"

Dorothea clapped her hand over her mouth and shook her head. "I can't tell you. Sorry, Edwina, I forgot you don't know."

"Hmmm, talk about being discreet," she teased. "Never mind, I heard nothing. If you and the chief are in on it, it will eventually come to light for the rest of us peons. Perhaps you should try those cookies out on the chief—keep him in a forgiving frame of mind."

"Very funny. I think I will though."

Chief Goodman was writing furiously at his desk when Dorothea tapped on his door.

"Mrs. Montgomery, come in. Well, now, what's this?" he asked as she set down the plate of cookies.

"These are the cookies the Guides are going to sell on Victoria Day. We're hoping to raise money for our summer camping trip. Help yourself. Tell me what you think."

"Mmm. I'm thinking you'll sell lots."

"You seem to be missing someone," she said waving towards the cell.

"Out on bail. Just writing up a report now. You missed the confessions of the lovebirds."

"Lovebirds?"

"Elspeth Roberts and Thomas Nathaniels."

"Really?"

"It seems your great-nephew George and Elva North got these two together to share what they suspected about one another and consequently two of my suspects gave a full statement this morning. At least I hope it's a full statement."

"And?"

He filled her in on how each saw the other come out of the suite at damning times and were fearfully suspicious but also determined to shield the other. He wrapped it up by saying, "I really don't think either of them did it. Well, most of me doesn't. I suppose they could be in it together. Either way it still leaves Mrs. Roberts as the most likely suspect. What I figure from the times that each saw the other, she could only have killed her husband between about 5:10 and 5:30."

"What about the break-in at the Wainfleets?"

"The break-in, yes. He's still on the hook for that and hasn't been forthcoming. I wrote to his superior. I'm hoping that'll flush something out. If he's hiding something, he still might be a murderer. Blast. They seemed so sincere this morning."

"So you didn't come up with a link between Nathaniels and Bill?"

"No," he sighed. "I need to go talk with him."

"Yes, I suppose you do. When are you going to let it be known that the "Nat" who people are getting to know at the bakery is one and the same as the military fellow who had been staying at The Imperial for several weeks? It's just that, well, people are inquisitive and may somehow work it out," she said, tilting her head.

"After I've heard from Colonel Brown."

"When do you think that will be?"

The chief considered. "Early next week I should think. Why?"

"Oh no reason. And, anyway, there'll be other things for people to think about. Where is Thomas now?"

"Back to work at North's Bakery."

"And Mrs. Roberts? Any further developments?"

"Not really. She doesn't hide her indifference towards her husband. She told me they were from Grand Portage, Minnesota, that Mr. Roberts had been in the lumber business on a large enough scale that he travelled into Canada with it, that Elspeth had adored her father. I have no solid evidence against her. Maybe she knows that and isn't worrying about being pinned with the murder. She certainly isn't saying anything to deflect suspicion from herself. She was seen walking when she said she was walking."

"But she wasn't seen with a walking companion, was she?"

"No."

"Does she know that Nat and Thomas are one and the same person?"

Chief Goodman rubbed his head. "That's a good question. I don't know."

"It may not matter, but then again maybe it does. What does Elspeth say about her mother?"

"She doesn't. I haven't asked her."

Dorothea raised her eyebrows.

"I'll ask. She better not be shielding her mother too."

Elspeth had returned to the North home after she and Thomas met with the chief. It had been her idea to send Mrs. North out for the groceries needed for Joe's favourite meal. It occurred to her that it might be a relief for Mrs. North to get out of the house and do regular things now that Joe seemed to be mending. Joe really didn't need round the clock care anymore but it seemed to set Mrs. North's heart at rest to know that Elspeth would be there. Had she known that her home was going to be a place for a police inquiry she might have been less willing to leave.

It was Joe who answered the door when the chief came calling.

"Well, now that does my heart good," said the chief, heartily shaking Joe's hand.

"And mine too, Chief. I can't tell you how sick I was of the four walls of my room. Haven't ventured yet outside of the house. At least I'm moving around *in* it though. But I'm itching to get back on the job. Although being in a state like this really shows who your neighbours are. I've had people come visit who I generally just nod to. One or both of the Wainfleets have checked on me faithfully every day even when I didn't know they were here."

"Every day?"

"Yep."

Chief Goodman perceived the faintest glimmer of hope. Talking to Bill Wainfleet just might not be as painful as he was reckoning on.

"I'm sorry to say I didn't come just to check on your welfare; I'm also here on official business," he said as he took a seat in the sunlit living room. "Glad to see too that you're out of the dark."

"You've no idea," said Joe grimly.

"I came to speak with Miss Roberts but I'm wondering …. is she here?"

"She's outside picking rhubarb."

"She won't be long then. How would you feel about taking up the questioning instead?"

Joe seemed to grow about two inches. "I'm sure I'd be up for it!"

"Right, I want you to question Miss Roberts about her mother's whereabouts in reference to Mr. Roberts' murder. I think she might be shielding her mother. She's done this once with Thomas Nathaniels—they're in love. But as far as I know they've both come clean. They were each holding back information that might incriminate the other. What a muddle. She'll be in shortly so I'll just say this much. I don't think it was either Miss Roberts or Mr. Nathaniels which leaves us with Mrs. Roberts. However, Mr. Nathaniels isn't entirely out of the soup because he still isn't telling me anything about that night you saw him around the Wainfleets' place. Be that as it may, at this point I just want to focus on Mrs. Roberts. If Miss Roberts is covering for her there must be something suspicious. Is that enough for you to go on?"

"Sure."

"Right. I'll just call Miss Roberts in and tell her you will be asking her some questions on my behalf."

Joe had decided to go for the assuming-what-we-suspect-to-be-true approach. "You can't continue to cover for your mother, Miss Roberts. In police circles that is considered obstructing justice," is how he started. It worked but it really got them no further ahead. Her evidence was a lack of evidence in that Miss Roberts had *not* seen Mrs. Roberts come out the front door of the hotel when she left for her walk but that was explained by the fact that she went out the back door. Of course, at this point they only had Mrs. Roberts' word for that: going out the back door, that is, because there were witnesses to confirm the actual walk. But Miss Roberts did pass along the theory that Elva had posited—that perhaps because Mrs. Roberts had not seen her daughter sitting in the library window as she was expecting, that the mother was shielding the daughter. When Chief Goodman read the note Joe had sent by a neighbourhood boy, he shook his head glumly and muttered, "There's just too much convoluted dancing around in this."

"Junior," he called from his office. "I need to talk to Bill Wainfleet and I sure hope I'll get a straight and easy answer. Then let's close up shop for the day and go fishing. We're likely to have better success with that than this case."

Chief Goodman took his fishing gear with him when he went to the station. He had every confidence that he would need that and not handcuffs. He leaned his fishing rod into a corner and poked his head through the ticket window.

"Hey, Bill. I was just over at Joe's. He was saying how much he appreciated you and Anna visiting so faithfully. Every day he said."

"Oh, sure. We just felt so bad 'bout him hitting his head right in front of our house. Thought maybe familiar voices would pull him out."

"Well, if it did I appreciate it too 'cause I've got him back on the job in an easy capacity. Just now I'm having him ask some questions about Mr. Roberts' murder."

"That's a bad 'un, that is. Glad it's your job and not mine. I was actually visiting Joe that evening. Thought for that bit of time Philip might like to be on his own. And I think he was right glad of it too. He just might shape up to take my place."

"Good to hear it, Bill, good to hear it. Nelson Jr. and I are off fishing. Need to rest my brain. Just wanted to thank you for helping to bring 'round my right hand man."

A train whistle blew in the distance. Bill pulled out his pocket watch.

"Right on time," he smiled. "Love it when it goes as it should."

"Me too," said the chief, retrieving his rod. "Me too."

Chapter Fourteen

By Friday, Dorothea was piling pots and pans and large spoons in a box and stuffing bunting around them. She topped it all with the grass skirts. This evening's parade to the ribbon cutting of Aunt Jane's, the new outhouse at the property, was to begin the festivities of the long weekend. It looked to be a peach of a weekend weather-wise which for the Victoria Day weekend was unusual. The present moment was May at its best— fresh, caressingly warm, bright, hopeful "the gladsome month of lively May." Birds caroled and swooped and the buds were swelling with gladness at being so close to their bursting forth. It seemed that the elements of each day of the week had been a little lovelier than the day before, all leading to the fullness of this day. But Dorothea, although she had kissed her hand to this beauty upon rising, was now deep in astonished thought and paying no attention to the day's balm. Here she was preparing for a quirky family celebration which now included two murder suspects—well, three, the third also suspected of breaking and entering. All people whose existence was unknown to her a month ago. Well, that wasn't entirely true in that the existence of the one was known to her but under a different name and persona. She was thinking back to the events of earlier in the week: the cricket practice, in particular, last evening.

She had heard the account from George about the meeting he and Elva had arranged with Elspeth and Thomas. The outcome of that, of course, was that

Elspeth and Thomas had made known to Chief Goodman their mutual withholding of information. Thomas was back at work at the bakery and Elspeth was enfolded into the North's family home. After working hours, the two of them were seen out walking, and Thomas tagged along with George to cricket practice. Mrs. Roberts was also seen walking—a lot. People didn't know what to say to her but her presence was acknowledged with a wave or nod of the head. Dorothea had been out walking Lily while Charles was at cricket practice and she caught sight of Mrs. Roberts standing on the edge of the cricket field. Squaring her shoulders, Dorothea had brought Lily to a standstill beside her.

"Good evening, Mrs. Roberts."

"Good evening. I can't make heads or tails of this game," commented Mrs. Roberts without preamble.

Dorothea laughed. "You wouldn't be the only one."

"It's fascinating though. I think I would like to play it."

"Really? Well. Are you sporty then?"

"Yes, I am. I think I mentioned when you visited us before—before my husband died—that I like to be active."

"You did, I remember. Are there particular sports you like more than others?"

"Tennis, swimming. I play on a women's softball team."

Dorothea had imagined how any of these pastimes might contribute to the strength needed to kill someone.

"And I also play in a marching band."

"What do you play?"

"French horn."

What had flashed through Dorothea's mind was the historical trivia that the French horn grew out of the shape of a hunting horn which, of course, has to do with killing things. *Get a hold of yourself,* she thought to herself. One can't pick out a murderer by the instrument they play. Although if they played it badly one might feel inclined ... *Stop it,* she again scolded. Like her fellow townspeople, she hadn't known what else to talk about so she had excused herself and continued on her walk.

But after cricket practice, Charles had trailed home with George and Thomas in tow. Talk turned to the events of the weekend with Charles describing Aunt Jane's parade. One thing led to another and George being a part of the family was, of course, included which meant Elva was included. From there Elva wanted to bring Elspeth and Elspeth in turn wondered if Thomas could come. Charles had seen Dorothea chatting with Mrs. Roberts and as they readied themselves for bed, Dorothea had told him of her short exchange.

"A French horn player!" Charles had commented. "Well, now that might be an entertaining addition to our parade."

"Charles, you can't be serious!"

"Why not?"

"Well ..."

"Innocent until proven guilty; isn't that an immoveable tenet?"

"Well, yes, but ... our grandchildren ..."

"Dorothea, you're being uncharacteristically illogical. She's hardly going to break out into a murdering spree surrounded by people. It's still possible she's innocent. Although admittedly, I can't quite see how."

From the moment that Mrs. Roberts accepted her invitation, Dorothea had had a sense of foreboding, or senses of foreboding as it diverged into two streams of thought. On the one hand she wasn't sure what she thought about including Mrs. Roberts in the celebration, and on the other hand she wondered if, in fact, she was overlooking something that she should be bringing to bear on Mr. Roberts' murder. The fact that Elspeth wasn't living with her mother didn't bode well on either front. Dorothea was feeling decidedly annoyed with Charles. It seemed to her that hospitality at the expense of the comfort of their grandchildren was taking things just too far. But he continued on his merry way of including Mrs. Roberts and had taken over a piece of martial music with a French horn solo that he thought would be just the thing for her to play as they proceeded to the outhouse. Although how that would fit together with the clanging and banging of the pots and pans was more than Dorothea could conceive of. She hoped Mrs. Roberts possessed a sense of humour or at least the ability to acknowledge the absurdity of it all. She hadn't displayed any particular sense of humour so far but to be fair, recent events weren't exactly conducive to humourous exchanges.

So here she was, looking ahead to the evening's festivities with what could only be described as astonished dread.

The plan was to eat supper early and divide the revelers into two cars. Betty and Dilman would travel with Dorothea and Charles, while their daughter, son-in-law and grandchildren would head out in their car. But now another car needed to be rounded up to carry their five extra guests. George was put on that detail. He hit on the idea of borrowing Edwin and Edwina's car which then led to the conclusion, by Edwina, that really such a festive occasion needed all vehicles to be adorned with bunting and more to the point, George and Elva should go in his two seater while she and Edwin would take Mrs. Roberts, Elspeth and Thomas with them.

"Dorothea will be glad to have someone else to help smooth over any awkward situation between mother and daughter," Edwina had announced.

So two more guests were added. Welcome ones to be sure but Dorothea was beginning to wonder if she should issue a town wide bulletin that all and sundry were welcome to the christening of their septic solution.

When the four grandchildren arrived, it was to the unexpected and exciting sight of two extra cars in Grandma and Grandpa's driveway and heaps of bunting ready for eager hands to drape the waiting vehicles.

By 6:30, the party guests were trundling out of town to the country property. It was only a ten minute drive, which, according to the inhabitants of the various vehicles, would either feel like ten seconds or ten hours. Edwina had strategically placed each of her occupants in the car.

"Thomas, here are a few pots for you to hold and you sit up here with Edwin," instructed Edwina. "His mother was a superb cook. Edwin can tell you of her culinary triumphs. If you ladies don't mind, I'd really like to sit in the middle as it helps me if I can see through the windshield while I'm back here. I get a wee bit queasy otherwise. Would you like me to hold your horn on my lap, Mrs. Roberts, or are you comfortable? Elspeth, do you mind holding the rest of the pots? I've got the spoons here. Edwin and I have done quite a bit of travelling in the States; maybe we have been to some of the same places."

And in such a way between talk of food and travel, the car carrying Willowsdown's trio of suspects wended its way to the parade.

Carting all their paraphernalia, the group met behind the small whitewashed house with apple green shutters, the home of the property's caretakers, Mr. and Mrs. Given. Charles gave instructions.

"Dilman, you lead the way with the handkerchief on the walking stick. Then, I think, Mrs. Roberts you come next with the horn. And then," Charles paused. He had caught his daughter Mary's eye and quick shake of the head which meant that the children wanted to be right at the front of the parade. "Actually, let's change that. We'll put you first," he said affectionately, moving to where his grandchildren, Leland, Magdala, Simon and Lucy stood. Leland and Simon were wearing the pirate hats they had shaped from paper and Magdala and Lucy were adorned with their grass skirts and paper crowns. All four expectantly held a pot or pan and spoon. Charles lay a hand lightly in turn on each child's headgear saying, "You four follow Dilman and then Mrs. Roberts if you would come in behind them?"

Mrs. Roberts nodded her head briefly. Dorothea couldn't interpret her expression.

"And then the rest of us?" piped up Edwina.

"Yes, just fall in as you like. I'll bring up the rear with my drum." As a youngster, Charles' father had played in a town band put together on a whim at the accession of Queen Victoria in 1837. His father had emigrated a year later at age 14 with his parents and brought the drum with him really for nostalgic reasons as it was rarely played. Charles had never seriously taken it up but he figured, how hard could it be? And, anyway, a drum was essential for such an event. Mary's husband, John, was an accomplished pianist but such instruments really didn't lend themselves to marching.

Earlier in the day, Mr. Given, had rigged up a ribbon across the outhouse. Dorothea carried the scissors and the bunting that would be strung amongst the trees that encircled Aunt Jane's once she was official.

"Ready, Ho! Off we go!" called Charles.

Nonsensically, George began singing, "We're Marching to Zion," and everyone joined in over the din of metal spoon on pots and pans, the mellow playfulness of the horn and the uneven beating of the drum. The distance to cover was about 300 feet, not so very far, but Dorothea did wonder whether the noise rendered during the interval would curdle the cows' milk in the neighbouring farmer's field.

The parading was accomplished without a misstep. Gathering in front of the small structure, Charles said, "I believe such a moment needs worthy words. Let me recite a little something from Robert Louis Stevenson." He straightened and cleared his throat.

"Bring the comb and play upon it!
Marching, here we come!
Willie cocks his highland bonnet,
Johnnie beats the drum.

Mary Jane command the party,
Peter lead the rear;
Feet in time, alert and hearty,
Each a Grenadier!

All in the most martial manner
Marching double-quick;
While the napkin, like a banner,
Waves upon the stick!

Here's enough of fame and pillage,
Great commander Jane!
Now that we've been round the village,
Let's go home again."

Applauding and laughter all around. Even from Mrs. Roberts. Dorothea cut the ribbon, and Charles announced the official opening of Aunt Jane's.

"And now," continued Charles, "the moment you've really all been waiting for!"

George and Dilman appeared from behind the outhouse carrying a baby's bathtub between them which was covered with straw.

"Now just give me half a minute," said Betty. "Children, help me here with getting rid of this straw."

"Just keep that," said Dilman. "You never know—it might come in handy."

The covering of straw had been to help keep the ice cool that was packed around the bucket of ice cream nestled within.

"Elva, open up that basket. There are a few blankets in there for laying on the ground and the cups and spoons and the peanuts and chocolate sauce. Be quick. This ice cream is already soft."

Within a very short time, the group was wiping the remains of the wondrous treat from their mouths. It had to stretch further than Betty had anticipated (which had caused a bit of a furor in the kitchen when the number of extra guests had been announced—not to mention the identity of some of them) but somehow everyone felt they had enough. Pots and pans and spoons and straw and all the other detritus of the event were gathered up and everyone began to wander back to the cars. Edwina and Dorothea walked together.

"That was gloriously fun!" exclaimed Edwina. "We need to come up with a reason to do it again—including the ice cream sundaes."

"The children would certainly be up for it," said Dorothea. They were racing ahead, banging and clamouring for all they were worth, shouting out their love of ice cream. "Maybe for Elva and George's wedding?" She tipped her head backwards to indicate the two who were lingering behind.

"So it's on again?"

"I believe so."

"Oh what fun!"

"And what do you think of the other two?" meaning Elspeth and Thomas who were sauntering a ways in front of them.

"Really?"

"I think so."

"But they just met!"

"Love at first sight ...apparently."

"Please tell me the chief still doesn't consider them suspects."

"In the murder, no, he's pretty sure not."

"You mean there's something else?"

"Possibly."

"But the only other thing is ... No! That doesn't make sense!"

"How was your drive in?" asked Dorothea, changing tack.

"Quite pleasant actually. You know, Dorothea, I don't see how any of them could have anything to do with Mr. Roberts' death. They all seem entirely normal even though it was admittedly stilted between Elspeth and Mrs. Roberts. Although there was a rather odd exchange. I can't even tell you how it began but at one point, Nat was saying that Chief Goodman had been told all. And then Mrs. Roberts said, 'All?' and Elspeth said—emphatically, I thought—'He knows I wasn't at the library and why, and he knows that Nat is Thomas.' There was a silence and then Mrs. Roberts said, 'Oh. I see it now.' What on earth were they talking about?"

"Mrs. Roberts said that?"

"Yes."

"Hmmm."

"Hmmm—what?"

"Grandma!" said a panting six-year-old Simon who had raced back to ask her a question. "Dilman says he has lots of stuff to make a fire with when we get back to your house if you say it's all right and Betty says she's got marshmallows we could roast. Please, Grandma?"

"And what does your mother say?"

Simon looked crestfallen. "I haven't asked her yet."

"It's fine with me if it's fine with her."

The easy half of the battle won, Simon headed toward his mother with hesitant exuberance.

Grateful for the distraction from a conversation that was heading in a direction that Dorothea couldn't continue, even with her best friend, she said smiling, "It would seem the evening is just beginning. Fire starting must be what Dilman had in mind about the straw."

Chapter Fifteen

Saturday was the day when dozens of the Girl Guide cookies from Mr. North's recipe and approved by Dorothea and various others would be baked in various homes of the intrepid Guides including Dorothea's in readiness for the bake sale on Monday which was the upcoming holiday of Victoria Day. Already the dough was being rolled out on the large kitchen table and cut into rounds. The grandchildren had been shooed outside to play. The task this morning was to scour the neighbourhood, and the town, if needed, to find suitable pieces of dry wood to feed the fire they were promised for that evening but when that was accomplished their contribution to the cookie manufacturing was to help count cookies into brown bags.

As the Guides' leaders, Dorothea and Edwina were quality control for the cookies. Later that morning when everyone who was preparing cookies had finished, the two women divided the "territory" and inspected the offerings. All was well including their own efforts so when Elva came into the Montgomery kitchen after lunch, Mary and the children were bagging the cookies.

"Hello, Elva," said Mary. "Are you here to help with the cookies?"

"No. But I can if you need help."

"No, no," laughed Mary. "As you can see the task is well covered."

"I actually came to speak with your mother," replied Elva, feeling shy.

"I think she might have popped over to Edwina's but she'll be right back if you'd like to wait."

Elva hesitated. "I think I'll head over there and see if I meet her on her way back."

"All right. If you should miss her, I'll let her know you're looking for her."

"Thanks," said Elva with a wave.

Dorothea was on her way back and Elva fell into step beside her.

"Mrs. Montgomery," she began.

"Is there not a reason to call me Aunt Dorothea?" Dorothea asked coyly.

Elva blushed. "Yes, there is."

"May I ask how that came about?"

"It was when George came to me on behalf of Thomas to ask if I would be willing to arrange for Elspeth to speak with Thomas and I was on my way to do the same on behalf of Elspeth. I realized I couldn't resist such a big-hearted man. And he paid Thomas' bail too. We did get Elspeth and Thomas together to talk but we talked first. He said he was sorry for not understanding about me wanting to work and he admitted he still really didn't understand it but he figured I knew what I was doing. His confidence in me touched my heart. We don't see eye to eye on everything but I think we have what it takes to work life through together."

"Honouring one another is a key ingredient."

"Thomas has said he wants to bake our wedding cake. He said he's a bit rusty as it's been awhile but if we're willing, he'd like to do that as a gift and a thank you."

"Elva, you do know that not everything is cleared up surrounding Thomas. The townsfolk still think of him as Nat Thompson. He's still under investigation by the chief. Something isn't quite right and he hasn't yet told everything he could tell."

"Oh. Joe hasn't said anything. Does Elspeth know this?"

"Joe can't say anything in his official capacity and as for Elspeth, I don't know," said Dorothea gently. "We all like him and I would be more than happy to know that he and Elspeth could make a life together but until Chief Goodman has cleared him of all charges, I think it would be best if you didn't build too much on the friendship. Have you agreed to his offer of the cake?"

"We didn't see any reason not to."

"Were you planning on continuing with your original wedding date?"

"No, that would be too soon. June 4 is only two weeks away. We're moving it to July 9."

"You've told your mother that Thomas will be making the cake?"

"Yes. What do you think I should do?"

Dorothea hesitated and then said, "I understand that something might come to light next week. If it is of a nature that would make us all unhappy then there is still time for someone else to make the cake. If not, then nothing has been lost."

"And I was just beginning to feel excited about all the preparation."

"Just enjoy George's company for now and we'll see what next week brings."

The bags of cookies were lined up in the pantry, the day had wound down to evening and the Montgomery household was sorting through the impressive array of branches and chunks of wood that the children had hauled home in what had been their uncle's wagon. There was even a small pile of wood shavings from the town's carpenter along with discarded newspapers and various letter type papers retrieved from the top of trash bins which were being crumpled as fire starters.

Dorothea was doing her share of crumpling, admittedly nosily reading a few of the letters. They were mostly of the thank you variety, a few newsy ones from family members. She was beginning to lose interest when her eye caught the phrase, "if it hadn't been for that man, I'm sure your father would still be alive today." That was not the garden variety kind of comment usually found in the prosings of a family letter. It ended, 'with love, Mama'. There was no date or address heading at the top. But there was a line that read, 'Very much looking forward to your visit.' An unhappy suspicion entered her head. *No*, she thought, *that is too much of a long shot.* She began to crumple the paper for throwing on the fire but held back. If it didn't apply where she thought it might then it was best to bring it into the open and confirm the injustice of her suspicion. But if the letter matched the circumstance …. She folded it and tucked it in the pocket of her cardigan. It would not be feeding this evening's fire.

Very early Sunday morning, Dorothea woke with a start from a dream about a giant roasting a marshmallow, except the marshmallow was so small that he couldn't really see it and so kept burning it which made him so angry that he would punch himself in the nose and then start all over again. Charles was breathing evenly beside her and as far as she could tell there was no smell of burning marshmallows. She lay on her back readjusting to reality and shaking her legs restlessly. She sighed and thought sadly about the implications of the letter she had found. Until it was verified, she ruminated, it could simply be one of those odd coincidences that do happen in life. She gazed at the shadowy ceiling not wanting to connect the dots that she was beginning to see before her eyes. Out of the corner of her mind another thought vaguely flitted–

–some memory connected to another piece of paper. She was on the edge of an epiphany but her nighttime brain was too slow to catch it and it dropped away. She sighed again. The letter would have to be given to Chief Goodman. Usually when she had a knotty question to untangle she made herself some cinnamon toast. She was sure it was conducive to charging up brain cells. That would mean though, getting out of bed and shuffling *all* the way to the kitchen, unwrapping the bread, toasting it to the perfect golden brown toastiness, buttering it right to the edges and then sprinkling it with a mixture of cinnamon and sugar also right to the edges and with just the right depth. She was the only one who could do it satisfactorily. If she wanted brain food it was up to her. It seemed like too much work at the moment so she would have to use the laying-in-bed-with-toes-pointed-and-arms-at-her-sides   method   for mulling things over.

With toes pointed, she brought her mind back to the letter. An idea crept in. Wouldn't it speak more loudly if the letter were kept silent? *Yes*, she thought it might. And Chief Goodman just might think so too. Hmmm ... yes. Pleased with herself and happy to have a plan of action, she rolled over, draping her arm across Charles' chest and soon matched her drowsing breath with his.

After a noisy noontime meal of the usual Sunday pot roast, Dorothea's daughter, son-in-law, grandchildren and Charles squeezed themselves into a car and drove out to the property—"The Estate" as George had dubbed it. After the ribbon cutting ceremony at Aunt Jane's, the children had spotted fish darting in the nearby creek and were eager to try their hand at catching them. Dorothea folded the letter into her purse and walked over to Chief Goodman's. She hoped she would find him still awake and not nodded off into a

Sunday afternoon slumber. Her knock was answered by Nellie.

"Hello, Mrs. Montgomery."

"Hello, Nellie. I'm sorry to disturb you but I need to speak with your father. I hope he isn't resting."

"Oh, no. In fact, he's mumbling over some paper work. I'll bet he'll welcome a distraction."

Chief Goodman looked up at the sound of their footsteps coming into the kitchen.

"Mrs. Montgomery! Am I glad to see you. Take a look at this."

On the table lay two sheets of paper. On the left-hand side of the first sheet she examined was a list of addresses in block letters and on the right was a rough map. On the map were small drawings that looked like buildings, tiny sketches of railway tracks, a couple of bridges and a large waterfall. The addresses each had a building, track or bridge sketch beside it. The second paper had a similar layout but the map seemed to include a body of water and obvious sketches of ships in a port along with the building, tracks or bridge sketch.

"Where did you get these?" asked Dorothea.

"They were in the papers we took from the Roberts' suite. It's just now that I've got to looking them over."

"Oh my," she murmured picking up one to look at it more closely. She pointed to an address on the paper with the falls. "Clifton Hill. That has to be Niagara Falls!"

"Yep."

"But where is this other one?"

The two of them bent closer to the paper.

"That little island there in the bay," said Dorothea, "it looks like it says, 'McNabs Island'."

"Halifax!" they exclaimed together. Since the horrific explosion in Halifax harbour in 1917 everyone knew the geography of the area.

"Interesting way to plan a trip. There must be points of interest at each of these marked spots," said Dorothea.

"Maybe," replied the chief dubiously.

"When I spoke to Mrs. Roberts on the day Mr. Roberts died, she mentioned that they were planning to travel to Niagara Falls but it didn't sound as though they were going any further east."

"I haven't shown you this yet," said the chief as he turned over each of the papers.

On the top left-hand corner of each, written in very small block letters were dates from the year before.

"Oh," said Dorothea, "but ... that doesn't fit with them travelling now."

"No, it doesn't."

"Now what?"

"I'll have to show them to Mrs. Roberts."

Opening her purse, Dorothea pulled out the letter she had kept back from the fire saying, "And I have to show you this."

"Did you think of anyone in particular?" she asked after he had perused it.

He nodded, saying slowly, "And you know it does make more sense. It occurred to me that maybe someone had hit Mr. Roberts. Punched him in the nose. The autopsy report indicated that if there had been such a blow it would have come from someone right-handed. In one of my talks with Mrs. Roberts I noticed her rubbing ink off her left hand. So she's left-handed. What do you think we should do with the letter?"

"I thought that rather than confronting him with it at first shot, it might prove more revealing if we see what happens after he hears about the death of Mr. Roberts."

"Yep," he replied after considering. "I think you're right."

That evening, Alex Kaminen and his mother disembarked at Willowsdown's train station. Bill Wainfleet was there as stationmaster to welcome them as well as George Flesherton and his mother, but Chief Goodman, with the letter in his pocket, was not.

Chapter Sixteen

Monday was another pearl of a day. The folk of Willowsdown took their Victoria Day celebrations seriously but at a leisurely pace. Sometime after lunch, those who had wares to sell set up along the sidewalk of one side of the main street. The parade was scheduled for 4:00 p.m. so there was plenty of time for sales before and during the parade. After the parade, everyone went home for supper. Then at dusk most of the town gathered in the park to ooh and ah over the fireworks. All in all, it was always a very satisfactory day.

New this year to the row of vendors was the Girl Guides' table and by 2:00 p.m. their cookie sales were in full swing. Dorothea had insisted on providing bite-sized samples as she was convinced that once would-be buyers had a taste, they would be sure to want to put their money where their mouth was. Whether or not it was the samples, the cookies were selling well.

"You know," said Dorothea to Edwina in a lull, "maybe we should do another round of selling in the fall. I wonder if taking the cookies *to* people would work? The Guides could go out in pairs and sell them door to door. What do you think?"

Edwina thought about it. "My dear girl, you just might be on to something."

Dorothea saw the Johnsons coming their way with their son, Chamberlain, who was home from college for the long weekend. There had been talk of a romance between Chamberlain and one of the town's girls but as Chamberlain and his mother had ambitions for him to attend Oxford, whatever tender feelings there might have been seemed to have been squashed. Coming out of The Imperial was Mrs. Roberts with Mary Goodman. Elspeth and Thomas had already bought their share of cookies. She hadn't yet seen Elva and George. Perhaps Elva had taken her advice and was putting distance between the couples. Considering that Elspeth was living in the same house, Dorothea wondered how she was doing that. Maybe the fact that Elva and George had been estranged for several weeks allowed her to use the excuse that they just wanted to be together to make up for lost time. Whatever the state of affairs, the two couples were evidently not wandering about together at the moment. And there was Mrs. Flesherton and her sister Mrs. Kaminen. Mrs. Flesherton was talking animatedly and pointing out town features. Mrs. Kaminen looked worn but what? At rest maybe? As though she had come through a struggle but was now still. Dorothea sighed. And there were the two cousins George and Alex. George was talking with the look of trying to remember salient details in bringing Alex up to speed on the business. The settling in of Mrs. Kaminen would be up front and centre in the minds of the family. In light of such a significant life change, the wider concerns of the town would come later in the conversation—even such a detail as Mr. Roberts' murder as he was, after all, a stranger. Her attention was restored to the task at hand when the Browns bought four bags of cookies. But it then wandered again as she was impatient to hear from Chief Goodman what Mrs. Roberts had to say about the papers they had examined yesterday. It was another 15 minutes before she caught sight of him leaving The Imperial.

"I told Mary I'd buy some cookies and let her enjoy a walk with Mrs. Roberts," he said, counting out a pile of change.

Dorothea handed him his bag of cookies at the far end of the table and said in a lowered voice.

"I noticed that Mary was with Mrs. Roberts today."

"I needed to be sure she was out of her suite."

"Oh?"

"I wanted to see if there was any correspondence we had missed: anything with block letters on it."

"And was there?"

The chief shook his head.

"And when you showed her the papers, what did she say?"

"She seemed genuinely surprised. She said she had no idea why her husband would have them."

Dorothea shrugged. "Do you think it matters?"

"Not sure. Probably not. Whatever it was about, the man is dead."

"Whatever else we don't know," stated Dorothea, "that, is an incontrovertible fact."

The parade did the town proud as usual. The school had a float as well as did a number of the businesses, one of the churches and the Women's Institute. The fire brigade loaded up the truck with its volunteers and the town's band was making a fine show of marching and playing in tune. Veterans from the town and surrounding areas rounded out the display. Seeing the former soldiers in uniform triggered a notion in Dorothea's mind. It was the inkling of the epiphany she couldn't catch last night.

"Leland, would Grandma be able to borrow your scooter?"

Her oldest grandchild, at nine, Leland used his scooter whenever he could, even bringing it with him when visiting his grandparents.

He looked at her incredulously. "Do you know how to use one, Grandma?"

"I think I can manage it. It's just that I need to get back to the house quickly. There's something I need to look at. I won't be long," she reassured him as he looked doubtfully between his grandmother and his scooter.

"Sure, Grandma." He knew his grandmother had never failed him. She likely had a good enough track record to be entrusted with the beloved scooter.

Except for Charles who took it in stride, her family stared unbelievingly as she set off with a fair bit of wobbling.

"Be right back. Will explain later!" she called, blowing a collective kiss.

Getting a rhythm going, she pictured where she had put it. She had been reading it at night, willing some twilight inspiration and had ... and had fallen asleep doing so. Likely it had fallen from her hand and slid under the bed. Yes. That would make sense. She was making good time on this thing. Maybe she should get one. She was quite proud of herself by the time she reached her door. *Not past it yet,* she thought. But then it came to stopping and that was not a movement of gracefulness. Leland made it look so easy. However, she was here. She puffed up the front porch steps, pushed open the door, sprinted (sort of) up the staircase and into her bedroom She could just see the edges of the manila envelope and the sheet of paper peeking from under the bed. She snatched up both and scanned the contents of the paper: geographical coordinates of bridges, train tracks, depots and roads in Vermont. It didn't make sense from a bootlegging standpoint but it did make sense if it was a sheet separated from a military report. Maybe a military report being copied out by a junior officer. A junior officer staying at The Imperial.

Chapter Seventeen

Chief Goodman, Dorothea, Elspeth and Thomas all missed the fireworks that evening. Dorothea had safely delivered the scooter back to Leland who had tried to hide his relief, and after locating Chief Goodman, Dorothea handed him the envelope saying, "bring the Roberts' papers and meet me at the station."

Chief Goodman looked up from reading the contents of the envelope and asked, "Remind me. Dianna found this in Thomas' room, right?"

"Right. When we were looking at it in terms of illegal alcohol sales we really couldn't make sense of it. But if we change the context, it has a similar feel to the papers from Mr. Roberts that we looked at yesterday, wouldn't you say?"

He nodded slowly. "I would indeed."

"Is it possible that they are connected? That Thomas killed Mr. Roberts for them and then couldn't find them?"

He sighed. "I really hoped I was done with Thomas as a suspect."

Dorothea raised her eyebrows and tilted her head.

"I'll call him in."

Dorothea, Chief Goodman and Thomas sat triangularly in the waiting area. Thomas was holding the document about Vermont in his hand as Dorothea spoke.

"This is what I think, Thomas. You were here in Willowsdown to copy a document. You had finished it and you were on your way to deliver it when you realized a page was missing. So you came back and that was the evening Joe North saw you."

"If you've been sworn to secrecy, son, I understand why you haven't been forthcoming, but it's out now. Clear your name and get on with your life," stated the chief.

Thomas began, tentatively keeping his eyes on the sheet of paper, "I've always been absent minded. Even while I was copying this, I'd sometimes mislay my pen or something and Elspeth would bring it to me. That's how we met. I had finished copying the document and was on the train taking it to the colonel. At one of the stops, I was leafing through the copy and realized there was a page missing. I had to find it. I got off at that stop and caught the next train coming back here. When I arrived, I searched the station. Then I thought maybe Bill Wainfleet had found it and took it home. When I saw that no one was home I went in." He stopped and looked up blushing. "My next idea was that it had slipped out somehow in my hotel room. Idiotically, I hopped on Mr. Wainfleet's bike to get me to the hotel quicker. That's when Joe North saw me."

Dorothea said, "It was at the hotel. Dianna found it while she was cleaning the room. She showed it to Mr. Schlessinger but he didn't think it was of any importance. She wasn't as sure so she brought it to me. We couldn't make heads or tails of it except that it was evidently part of a whole. I kept it on the off chance that someone would come looking for it; maybe it was part of someone's project."

"It is that, Mrs. Montgomery. I still don't feel I can in good conscience break my oath of silence," he said, addressing Chief Goodman. "As you have written to Colonel Sutherland Brown, it's likely he'll tell you and I'd rather it came from him. Suffice it to say, it is a page from a government report that is classified information and of immense national significance."

The trio sat in silence.

"Is that why you came back in disguise—the dyed hair, moustache and glasses?" asked Dorothea. "You were still hoping to find it?"

"Yes."

"But you couldn't tell Elspeth."

"Given the job I was doing, uh, which as I said I'll leave to the colonel to tell you, I was torn for a bit in how I felt about Elspeth but when I returned, I realized I wanted to marry her and once I cleared up the mess I'd made, I decided I would quit the government job. Being hired by Mr. North was incredibly good luck."

Chief Goodman handed the other two papers to Thomas.

"What can you tell me about these?"

Thomas studied them and looked up slowly. "I would say these are the work of a spy. Where did you find them?"

Neither Dorothea nor Chief Goodman answered. They sat regarding him intently.

"Not Mr. Roberts!"

Chief Goodman inclined his head.

Thomas stood, handing all the papers back to the chief.

"I have worked for the Canadian government in a secret operation but, as God is my witness, I did not kill Mr. Roberts. If he was a spy, I knew nothing of it."

The three were silent again, the two seated regarding the one standing and the standing one unwaveringly meeting their gaze.

"Well," said Chief Goodman finally as he too stood. "At this point I'm going to consider this case closed as far as it concerns you. I want Colonel Sutherland

Brown's confirmation of your story though before I write it up officially."

"Thank you, sir. Your confidence means a lot."

"And Elspeth?" queried Dorothea.

"I'll tell her everything. She'll have to decide what she thinks of me in light of it all. I'll still leave my government position and stay in town no matter what. Not sure, though, how I'm going to explain my disguise to everyone." He sighed. "All this cloak and dagger stuff isn't for the likes of me."

After Thomas left to give his whole story to Elspeth, Dorothea and the chief looked at each other and shook their heads.

"Who would have thought?" said Chief Goodman.

"Do you think Mrs. Roberts knew about her husband?"

Chief Goodman groaned. "Who knows? I'm not cut out for cloak and dagger stuff either."

Mid-morning the following day, Chief Goodman was just thinking of heading to North's bakery to ask Thomas how he stood with Elspeth when the station door opened. He stood up from the seat in his office and nodded to Nelson Jr. who was doodling on a pad of paper at the counter. The nod meant two things: be ready for action and more mundanely, be ready to take notes.

"Good morning, Alex."

The big man stood uncertainly in the doorway.

"Come into my office."

Removing his hat, Alex followed the chief.

"I was hoping you would come to us."

"George just told me that the American fellow is dead."

"Which American fellow?"

"Well, Mr. Roberts."

"I understand that you knew him."

Alex nodded. "Yes. He did business with my father."

"And your mother believed that he was responsible for your father's death."

Alex looked surprised. "Yes."

"That's why you paid him a visit the day he died?"

"In a way. I was hoping I could convince him that morally he owed my mother some compensation. He deliberately put the mill into bankruptcy because he had invested in another one and didn't want the competition. He lied to our suppliers and customers and eventually the orders dried up. My father was heartbroken. Obviously, I can't with certainty attribute Mr. Roberts' actions to my father's death but he was so shocked and humiliated and seemed to lose the will to live. If there hadn't been a heart attack I think he would have, I don't know, faded away. My mother was left bereft financially and emotionally. I didn't realize that the American fellow who was staying at the hotel was Mr. Roberts until I happened to meet him in front of The Grocery Emporium. I was so surprised to see him I didn't think about confronting him. But once I knew it was him I decided to appeal to his compassion for a widow. He had none," finished Alex bitterly.

"How did you kill him?"

"Kill him!" exclaimed Alex. "I didn't kill him. I punched him. I was so angry at his indifference I just socked him. He hit his head against a corner of the mantelpiece. He kind of staggered around and then slumped into a chair. He pulled out his handkerchief to stop the bleeding of his nose. If he had stood, I would've hit him again but I couldn't hit a man who was sitting. He said, 'I could bring a charge of assault against you.' I said, 'Go ahead.' And then I left."

"What time was that?"

"I don't rightly know but I had delivered the meat to the kitchen. The young fellow who was taking over my route was with me so I left him to talk with the kitchen staff. I figured if I was going to talk to Mr. Roberts I'd best do it right then before I went away. It must have been shortly after 5:00 p.m. I was certainly on my way from the hotel before 5:30.

Chief Goodman considered the man in front of him. The townspeople good naturedly referred to him as the gentle giant and he did fit the description. From what the chief knew of him, Alex would champion his mother and certainly a punch from him would send a man reeling. Mrs. Montgomery had been right in her assessment of Alex's character. She believed that once he heard about the death of Mr. Roberts, he would come forward so that no one else would be wrongly punished. That's why she had suggested that the letter, which she guessed to be from Mrs. Kaminen, not be put to use, as it were, unless Alex failed to live up to their expectations. Alex's description of the events of that day could definitely fit the evidence that had been left behind.

Likely no one would ever know what exactly happened but Chief Goodman put his imagination to work. The blood flecks on the mantelpiece and on the wall behind it would fit the scenario of someone being punched in the face. It was possible that after Alex left, Mr. Roberts made his way upstairs to clean himself up. He was bleeding from a head wound and from his nose. That would account for the drops of blood found on the steps to the second floor. At the top of the staircase Mr. Roberts, who had been drinking heavily according to several witnesses, and now had a head injury lost his footing and fell backwards down the steps breaking his neck. Then in comes his daughter who finds her father dead. She had seen Thomas coming out of the suite just after 5:00 p.m. and assumed he had killed her father so she wipes down all traces of blood leaving damp spots and a washed out towel, handkerchief and dress.

Mr. Roberts had had a busy afternoon what with Thomas trying to talk to him about Elspeth and no sooner did he leave but Alex shows up and wants to have it out with him about his mother. He punches the man leaving him injured but alive. After cleaning up, Elspeth also leaves. And then Mrs. Roberts comes home and finds her dead husband after having been out for a walk just as she said.

It was all entirely plausible and as far as he could see fit the pieces of the puzzle as they knew them. So, in fact, no one had murdered Mr. Roberts. Except for his own admission, there was nothing to connect Alex to the scene. Chief Goodman had always been one to believe that police work had as much to do with reading character and probabilities as it had to do with facts and evidence. If Mr. Roberts' death didn't happen something like he had just imagined, he really did not have solid enough evidence to convince anyone that it happened differently—that for instance someone killed him in cold blood.

Mrs. Montgomery had been sad on a number of counts when it looked as if Alex was the murderer. One was the grief upon grief that would fall on his mother. Another was the sad horror felt whenever someone takes their sorrow and anger out in such a brutal and irreversible way. In addition, the loss of a person you thought you knew is a distress in itself. She would be happy to know that she was wrong to link Alex with murderous rage, happy that their gentle giant was still just that—well, mostly gentle anyway.

The letter was waiting for him when he came into work the next morning.

"Here, Dad," said Nelson Jr. holding out the official looking envelope.

Pouring a coffee from the pot on the stove Chief Goodman took his seat and hoped to hear from the Colonel something that would match Thomas' account.

Dear Chief Goodman,

Your letter has taken me by surprise. Thomas Nathaniels is one of our most promising officers and I can't reconcile what I know of him to the charges you have placed on him.

Thomas was in your town to make a copy of an official document that outlined a reconnaissance mission into the state of Vermont as a pre-emptive strike against a State side invasion of which we have had positive information. This is further to previous reconnaissance missions in 1921 and 1924. The information Thomas was copying referred to the latest mission in 1926.

Obviously this is information I am trusting you to keep absolutely to yourself. I only share it with you in light of the serious charges against Mr. Nathaniels. If you are looking for a character reference in a court of law you may count on my cooperation.

Sincerely,

Colonel James Sutherland Brown

The exchange connected him to the Montgomery house where Dorothea picked up the phone she had admittedly been hovering near in the hallway.

"Good morning, the Montgomerys'."

"Morning, Mrs. Montgomery. Nelson here. I have the letter from the colonel. I can't give you all the details but what he has to say confirms what Thomas has told us."

"I'm so glad! What a relief."

"Do you buy your bread sliced?"

"Pardon?"

"Dealing with this case has reinforced the truth that life is short. Some things aren't worthwhile spending time doing. Mary spends a lot of time slicing bread when she could be doing something else. I'm going to tell Mr. North that his bakery would benefit from a bread slicing machine. I know someone will slice it for you at the bakery but think of all the time everyone would save if they could stuff a loaf in a machine and have it come out ready to use."

Dorothea laughed merrily. "You're a good man, chief. By all means, give the woman sliced bread."

Chapter Eighteen

Two weeks later, Dorothea sat looking over the small group of people gathered in the restaurant at The Imperial. They were finishing a brunch that followed the morning wedding ceremony of Elspeth and Thomas Nathaniels. Dorothea smiled to herself. It wasn't so long ago she had been mournful that June 4 would not be a wedding day as Elva had broken off her engagement to George. And yet here they all were at a wedding on the very day—just not the marriage of Elva and George.

It had all come together very quickly. The Wainfleets were given a vague explanation as to why their house had been entered uninvited. They hadn't been overly concerned about it anyway as nothing had been taken and Bill's bike had never been far from home. So all charges against Thomas were cleared. There really wasn't anything that could be charged against Alex except perhaps assault but what was the point? Not even anything about causing grievous bodily harm as no one could say for sure if it was Alex's punch or the drinking that may have contributed to Mr. Roberts tumble down the stairs. Alex's explanation of his presence in the Roberts' suite that afternoon put everyone in the clear. With nothing criminal hanging over their heads and since not long ago eloping had seemed as good a way to start married life as any other, Elspeth and Thomas decided they might as well marry as soon and as simply as possible.

Mr. Schlessinger, the hotel manager, was so thankful to have his hotel free of all criminal activity that he offered the use of the restaurant and the brunch as a wedding gift. George and Alex contributed the sausage and bacon and the Finnish pancakes and Mr. North provided the bread and rolls along with Elspeth's new favourite dessert—empire cookies. Edwina was a whiz with a sewing machine so she whirled out a wedding dress for Elspeth and a bridesmaid's dress for Elva. Mrs. Brown scoured the countryside for the final remnants of lilacs and even a few forget-me-nots which Elspeth wanted in honour of her father. It had been agreed that since the new couple would be making their home in Willowsdown that nothing would be said to her about Mr. Roberts' rotten dealings with the Kaminen lumber mill. Alex and Mrs. Kaminen knew that Elspeth was not at all responsible for any of their family's tragic results. Let Willowsdown be a fresh start for all of them. And for their honeymoon, Charles was lending them his car to toodle around the countryside.

"It's only for a week," he had said. "Everything we need is in town and if I'm desperate to go somewhere further, faster, I'll get a horse from Everett Brown's stable."

Dorothea paused in her musings to welcome Mrs. Roberts to a seat beside her.

"It's all come together beautifully, hasn't it?" said Dorothea.

"It has. It's been so busy I haven't had the opportunity to thank you for how you helped both Elspeth and Thomas. I understand you had a key role to play. Although … there seem to be some gaps in the explanations that they've given me. Further to that I was surprised that Thomas gave up his military position. It would seem to be a career that would have a more expansive future than baking in a small town. Did something go wrong, do you think?"

Dorothea laughed in what she hoped was a carefree way. Chief Goodman had never fully told her what was in the letter from Colonel Sutherland Brown which meant it was classified information. It did make it a little awkward though to fully explain Thomas' behaviour.

"I think it only went wrong in the sense that he began in a less suitable career and has ended up in a thoroughly suitable one. In fact, one of the reasons they are taking a short honeymoon is that he wants to get back to start work on Elva and George's wedding cake. I hope …"

"I hope," Mrs. Roberts jumped in as though she were finishing Dorothea's thought, "he doesn't regret it. He did come back in disguise. That was a bit odd, don't you think? Was that ever explained to you?"

"I'm quite sure you don't need to be concerned about Elspeth choosing Thomas. I believe him, as do many others, to be a man of character. And what about you? Are you still planning on leaving us tomorrow?"

"Yes. It's time I began to make my way back home. Those two don't need me to help start their lives together. Despite everything, I've enjoyed my visit here. I've certainly come to know the prettiest areas in which to take a walk."

"You found the path through the old apple orchard then?"

"I did. What did you say the name of those apples were?"

"Northern spies. All the pie makers use nothing else. You'll need to come back in the fall when all the pies are being made."

"Yes. Yes, that might just be the right time to come again."

"So Charles," began Dorothea the following evening. They were sitting on their front porch very late indeed. Dorothea was savouring a perfectly executed cinnamon toast. "Not quite a month ago I was wondering about returnings. I was wondering if Elva and George would return to one another and whether the person who had misplaced the sheet with random information about Vermont would come back to find it. And in both cases, they have."

"Very satisfactory," replied Charles sleepily.

"Yes, very. And that curious sheet of paper has given us Elspeth and Thomas. And," she stopped chewing suddenly. "She said she was visiting Niagara Falls before heading home. That was on the map the chief found."

"Who?"

Dorothea was thinking back to the conversation with Frances Roberts at the wedding. Perhaps her concern in Thomas leaving the military had a different meaning. It didn't have to do with Thomas' character at all but with his knowledge: his knowledge of military secrets. His knowledge of people who might have or might want to have access to military secrets. Was she fishing to find out if he had come back because he suspected something?

Dorothea muttered to herself, "Chief Goodman said 'she was genuinely surprised that he had the papers.' She would have been. It wasn't Mr. Roberts who had recorded those places and made sketches and drawn a map. He must have found the papers and wondered what they were all about. It had nothing to do with him. She must have been frantic to know where they were. She obviously never realized that he had discovered them and that after his death they had been cleared away by the police."

"Dorothea, what are you talking about?"

Dorothea finished chewing and then swallowed the mouthful of cinnamon toast. It must have been her faithful cinnamon toast that charged up her deducing brain cells.

"I invited Mrs. Roberts back in the fall for apple pie but she can't be allowed back."

"Why not?"

" It was she who was the northern spy."

THE END

ABOUT THE AUTHOR

 Elizabeth Jukes has always enjoyed reading. Often, as a child, she would hold up a book to the slice of light from the front porch lamp that the not quite closed bedroom curtain allowed in. All this, of course, when she was supposed to be asleep.

Love of reading translated to love of writing. A Journalism Diploma followed, as well as a Bachelor of Theology, and then, with life's twists, many years of no writing except for journaling. But a few years ago, the Dorothea Montgomery character and Dorothea's town of Willowsdown appeared in her mind and the desire to flesh that all out in the Dorothea Montgomery series was irresistible. She hopes this series will tempt people to read beyond their bedtimes.

Elizabeth lives in New Hamburg, Ontario, with her husband, Jon.

AUTHOR'S NOTE

To any readers who might be wondering, Colonel James Sutherland Brown was a real person and the events he refers to in his letter did, in fact, take place. (As far as I know there was no Thomas Nathaniels involved.) More details can be found on Google but are more engagingly outlined in Pierre Berton's book, *Marching As to War*. Also historically true was the headline of May 7, 1927, to which Dorothea casts her mind. And, of course, Rocco Perri and Al Capone were real people as were the illegal alcohol goings on alluded to in the book.

Mrs. White's Apple Pie

Crust
2 1/2 cups flour
1 tsp. salt
1 cup lard (the best is from the Brown's farm)
1/2 cup water
1 T. vinegar
1 egg

Mix flour and salt in a large bowl. Cut in lard. Work into a coarse meal. Whisk together water, vinegar and egg and add this mixture a bit at a time until dough just hold together. Never overwork!

Filling
Peel and chop 7 cups worth of Northern Spy apples. Combine 1 T. flour, 3/4 cups sugar, 1 T. cinnamon and some dashes of nutmeg and cloves. Mix with apples until coated.

Assembly
Preheat oven to 425 degrees. Roll out pastry and line an 8" pie plate. Place apple mixture in crust. Dot with 2 T. butter. Cover with top crust. Make slits or outline an apple to let out steam. Bake at 425 degrees for 15 minutes. Reduce heat to 350 degrees and continue baking until apples are tender, usually about 40-45 minutes. Cool on side board.

www.ingramcontent.com/pod-product-compliance
Lightning Source LLC
Chambersburg PA
CBHW020335260626
47156CB00004B/1531